I0761915

Harvest of Hearts

Margaret Nyhon

Willow Press

Published by Willow Press
Author contact: margaretf@hotmail.co.nz

A catalogue record for this book is available from the National Library of New Zealand.

ISBN 978-1-0670438-2-7 (Hardback)
ISBN 978-1-0670438-3-4 (EPUB)

Contents

From the parents came the daughters,
from the vines came the grapes,
then came the fine wines.

Splendid isolation

ALANA WAS one of three daughters; her sisters Willow and Briar were older than her by one hour. Although they were triplets, they each had their own personalities, but this had no bearing on the nature of each child. Alana felt she was the less attractive of the three girls, thus believing she needed more attention from her parents, who did not for one moment think this was necessary. To them, the three girls were loved equally. They did have sneak thoughts about the future, and talked about the girls and how they would turn out; would these thoughts always prevail?

The girls loved the environment they were living in: they were privileged, but being young this was not a consideration. They caught the school bus at the end of their property but had to walk a kilometre to reach the pick-up point. Although they lived on a vineyard, it was different to all the neighbours, being not open to the public, and in fact anyone entering the property had to have permission. It was a wholesale winery, with no tastings or door sales. Their grandfather had planted the early vines, about four acres, and their father just kept buying land and developing it. Now they had seventy-five full-time staff, at least ten tractors and ten staff vehicles, not to mention all the necessary machinery to run the property.

Their father was a true entrepreneur, putting time into promoting his wines overseas, so he was away a lot of time. He wanted to establish as many overseas outlets as possible, because he could see in the near future the country being flooded with wines, with all the new wineries being established. Also, many 10-acre blocks of land were being planted in grapes for the owner's own consumption, so he identified this also as a looming problem. New Zealanders could not possibly consume all the wine the country produced. He had the foresight to establish overseas connections. He had studied to become a viticulturist in Adelaide, Australia and was one of the first from New Zealand to do so, which gave him the edge over the newbies. He was totally dedicated to his vineyard, and it had become his whole life, a dream come true. He could visualise acres of plantings on his land, even buying neighbouring properties to extend his dream. It was never-ending.

The private vineyard, at the end of a road, was something of a mystery around the district. Children were children, no one was any different to the next, but not so with the adults. There was much speculation as to who these people were; they appeared to be a little different to most of the locals. The girls did their schooling locally, until it was time to start senior school, then decisions had to be made as to where they wanted to attend. Of course, each girl had a different opinion, so this had to be sorted out. Their parents thought boarding school for their secondary education, to give them a feel for life outside their property, to let them experience the world.

After a lot of discussion, the two eldest decided on the same boarding school, but Alana chose to be different. She wanted to be separated from her sisters, as she felt there would be no more comparisons when she was away from them. As eager as the sisters were to choose their colleges, they would miss the comforts of their home life, but while being caught up in the excitement, this was forgotten. All they could see was new friendships, fun and no parental control.

Now it was their last month at home before leaving for boarding school. They all knew how to drive tractors as they had sat on their father's knee while he was doing tractor work, so he encouraged them at a young age to learn how to drive. Briar was the one who felt most at home in the shed with the machinery. They all wanted to come home in the future and be part of the vineyard. Their parents were big on conservation so the whole family spent many hours planting native shrubs and trees along the waterways on their land. In fact, it was Alana who wanted to become involved in horticulture, as this was her favourite job. She had pottles of seedlings stashed in the garden shed, hoping one day her father might invest in a little nursery so she could grow her own natives for future plantings. It was as if she knew her father's aspirations to own more land one day.

On their land was a walnut plantation which had been planted many years ago. It was fenced off into four paddocks and this was home to their black pigs. The parent pigs were in a paddock of their own and the little piglets were in a separate paddock. They produced the best pork and bacon simply because the pigs ate the walnuts as they fell from the trees, giving the pork a nutty taste. The family were spoilt for food, as most of it was grown on their own land, including the beef cattle and sheep. How long would it take the girls to realise how special their home life was? Perhaps boarding school was the best experience to make them realise how different their lives would be. It was called learning by experience!

The girls were making the most of their last couple of weeks at home. Briar was doing tractor work with Thomas. She spent most of her time in the workshop questioning him on the workings of the machinery, as anything with a motor drew her attention; she was a real tomboy. She had her own tool kit and her favourite person outside of the family was Thomas, the mechanic. Briar followed him around as his shadow, his sidekick, his apprentice, all of the above. She knew where every tool was in the workshop and even when Thomas tried to catch her out, she was one-step ahead of him. She was the jeans and overall girl; fashion was not a word in her vocabulary, but suggest going to a tool shop or a garage and she was first off the block. So, it was not surprising to find her in the truck as soon as a trip was needed to pick up spare parts or replace something old for something new. Could she survive at boarding school? This was going to be a real test, as she was the one most likely to feel a misfit. Especially having to give up her overalls for a school uniform. Perhaps at the weekends she could slouch around in overalls, but only time would tell.

Father's return

TODAY THEIR FATHER had just returned from his annual pilgrimage to Ireland. He would fly over with a keg of wine which travelled as freight, to serve at several pub tastings. This was his entrepreneurial skills kicking in, as Ireland was one of his most important markets. The labels on the wine bottles depicted the story of his ancestors' a notorious, scandal-filled past, which no one but the Irish would understand. The visit was expected by the Irish, so he chose to look after those that supported him and bought his wines. Perhaps it was the dollar signs that spurred him on, as to be a good entrepreneur one had to make sure the dollars were flowing in. It was one thing to be generous, but that didn't necessary bring in the money.

As much as he missed being away from his vineyard and his family, he had trained confident managers of each department who he trusted, so his business just kept flourishing. Most of his staff had been with him right from the start, so this was recommendation in itself. He was a good boss and treated his permanent workers like extended family.

Tonight was the last supper for quite some time, as in two days the girls were leaving the comfort of their own beds for a totally different environment. Excitement was mixed with apprehension: there was no going back! Their first break to come home was mid-term, but Easter was a week before, so it was decided to wait until mid-term. They were dining out at their parents' favourite restaurant so were encouraged to choose what they wanted. In two days' time choices would not be available. Willow and Briar were off to Diocesan School for Girls and Alana chose Epsom Girls Grammar School. But tonight, it was their choice, so they ordered their favourite dishes. There was plenty of talk about their selected colleges, although Alana was very quiet. Was it because she was going to be on her own, or was it because she was leaving her seedlings? Who would look after them, who would water them but most importantly, who would talk to them?

Willow and Briar chose their college because it was a prestigious private school with strong academic and extracurricular programmes and promoted excellence. Because they were competitive, each wanted to excel in their chosen subjects. Willow was the more study driven, as she wanted to follow in her father's footsteps to become a skilled viticulturist. One day she hoped to become the head winemaker of her father's estate. This meant she had to obtain high marks to attend the college in Adelaide for future winemakers. This all sounded like hard work for Alana, so she opted for Epsom Girls Grammar because it fostered personal responsibility, courage, compassion and a community-minded and caring society, and she knew she was not as bright as her sisters. This is why she felt she needed to live separate from them, so she could find her own self-worth. Tomorrow was the beginning of three new lives.

With their suitcases packed and loaded into the Range Rover, the first stop on their journey was boarding the inter-island ferry from Picton. When they reached Wellington, they would drive to Masterton and stay the night before journeying on to Auckland the following day. There was much discussion with their parents on remembering all the tasks each girl had left them to attend to, as this was goodbye to their old life, as such. The first drop-off was Alana at Epsom Girls. As her suitcase was lifted out of the boot, her sisters hugged her and said their goodbyes. They told her to come and visit them across the city anytime, should she need their company. Now it was her mother and father's time to say goodbye to the youngest of the triplets. Tears were shed as goodbyes were said, especially by her mother, while her father managed to hold on to his. "Remember, Father, to water my plants and seedlings; don't let them die," she gently told him. He came forward and gave her a hug. "Goodbye, Alana, take care and email your mother and me each week." There was the toot of the horn, and they were off to their next drop-off.

Willow and Briar were next. They were polar

opposites. Willow was dressed in a fashionable outfit while Briar was in a pair of dress overalls. As they lifted out their suitcases and put them on the asphalt, the goodbyes started again. Mother was in tears, even Father shed a tear as his sidekick was leaving him. Briar was always at his side, and he would miss her dearly, but he knew this day had to come. After the final goodbyes, the Range Rover gave a final toot and drove away. The girls wheeled their suitcases up to the main hall to do their check-ins and receive their allocated rooms. A new life was about to begin, not just for the girls but for the parents also.

Mid-term break

THE GIRLS WERE happy to be home again after six months at boarding school. The school food was the biggest hurdle, as mass-produced food was nothing like they experienced at home. Choices had disappeared and was replaced by bulk production of bland meals. Alana had found it hard to settle in as she missed her plants, so a lot of her time was spent in the school grounds. She had made friends with the young gardener, and he was only too happy to have company, as not many of the girls took any notice of him. His name was Timothy, and this was his first job, having just finished school the previous year. The older gardener had been here for forty years, so he stayed on to teach Timothy what to do. Now he was on his own among so many girls where he felt out of place, but he needed a job so he could help his elderly parents. He was beginning to enjoy the flower beds and Alana could help him with plant names, so they became good friends. She preferred his company to the childish girls at the school.

The happiest to be home was Briar as she missed her father and Thomas. A whole lot of silly girls' chatter was nothing compared to the man's talk in the workshop. Now she could get into her work overalls and go to her favourite place, among the machinery and with Thomas. She hadn't realised how much she missed him until she was back with in his company again. Although she knew he was a married man, she never thought about that. He was just Thomas to her, and they had formed a work-related friendship. He recognised the change in her; she was growing up and this worried him a little, and he hadn't realised how much he would miss her.

Alana had strong words with her parents as her plants had not been cared for the way she hoped they would be. They were not as passionate about them as she was, so she decided to plant the ones that had survived and not worry about cultivating any more, because they would not be looked after to her standards. Instead, she would study, reading native plant books. She didn't mind boarding school; she had made a couple of new friends and was working on finding out who she really was. It was in her alone time, when no one was around, that she was beginning to make headway.

Nothing was a worry to Willow who loved company and had sorted out friends with the same interests as herself. She was at college to study and do well, but this didn't mean she couldn't enjoy life. Her group of friends loved to leave the college grounds at weekends and explore life outside, with the most popular event walking past the boys' college and being wolf-whistled at. It gave them a buzz and something to laugh about. Now that she was back home, it was time to get out into the vineyards and talk with the workers. She loved to watch the vines start from bare branches, then the leaves would appear, and next little bunches of fruit formed, which was when she started to get excited. She had watched this cycle repeat itself each year and knew this was where her heart belonged, without doubt. Her thoughts never wandered; they stayed in the vineyard among the vines. But it was what happened to the grapes once they were brought through the doors into the winery itself that excited her above all else. The huge shiny vats full of wine burned a fire in her belly. She wanted to be the one who created what filled those vats. Their wine had not quite reached the point of being a top-selling wine, but it wasn't far away. Willow felt with her passion that one day she would make it to the top. This was her dream and like her father she held on to that. Dreams were meant to be more than just dreams; they had to be turned into reality.

Among the vines today were the workers from Vanuatu. They were doing the shoot thinning, removing excess shoots to allow the vines to focus on producing quality fruit. Leaf removal was also being handled to improve the airflow and to allow sun exposure, reducing the risk of disease. This was called canopy management. The vineyard covered so many acres that a large group of seasonal workers were needed. The workers from

Vanuatu were good steady workers and came back each year.

Willow's father believed in the area in which they had established their vineyard; the soil was suitable as was the climate. The property bounded a river, so the drainage was excellent as was the sunlight. All the flat area and the gentle rolling land was in vines. The rest was farmed and had a stock manager to look after it.

The girls had only ever known their life on the vineyard as it was discussed over breakfast, at the lunch table and again at night. Their father had instilled in them how fortunate they were to have a love for the land and what it could yield. The passion was there right from the start, and each knew, one day they would be the next generation to carry on the family legacy. It was fortunate they had interests in different areas, but all related to the running of the vineyard.

Seven years on

WILLOW HAD GRADUATED from the University of Adelaide as a qualified viticulturist and was now back home on the vineyard. This was the beginning of her dream; her next ambitious step was to create an award-winning wine. Every day she was walking among the vines testing the grapes as they began to soften and change colour. This depended on the type of grape, green to purple for the red varieties, and translucent for the white. Sugar levels were important, for as these levels increased, it decreased acidity and that was the beginning of the flavour developing. This was a crucial time as these levels had to be perfect to make a stand-out wine. This was where it was won or lost! Sugar levels and flavour profiles were tested regularly to determine ripeness. Of course, at this time the pesky birds were starting to flock in, so decisions had to be made on when to roll out the nets.

Up until now Willow had had a free run on the

decision, but the three sisters had to cooperate, as each had a part to play in their separate fields. Alana was testing the soils and looking for signs of pests and diseases, and this would be compromised by the nets, so she asked Willow to leave the nets until the last possible moment. This annoyed Willow as she had a deadline to arrange for staff to roll out the nets. The girls knew they had to respect each other's expertise as their father had mentioned; he could foresee problems if they took matters into their own hands. They had been warned loud and clear that respect had to prevail, but would this be so?

Briar, on the other hand, was the tomboy sister and her interest in the mechanical and problem-solving side of things, in the day-to-day operations, were crucial. She ensured, along with Thomas, that the tractors and harvesters as well as the motor vehicles were in good shape and ready to go when needed. Thomas was still the head mechanic, but now that Briar was also a qualified mechanic, she had the sense to know that his knowledge was invaluable to them and, besides, she secretly admired him. It had only surfaced since she came back home full-time, as while at college she missed him but did not understand why. Being that much older and a little wiser, her feelings were surfacing, and Thomas was right up there at the top of them. She knew he was a married man but had no children. She thought he liked her as she had seen him out the corner of her eye studying her. This made her all the more interested, although there was roughly a fifteen-year difference in their ages, but this didn't deter her as she found him comforting and easy to get on with. He was always playing pranks on her and this she found playful. Was it a message?

What the girls didn't see, their father did, or thought he did. Here were three very wealthy heiresses to be with not a worry in the world, so what an invitation to a luxury lifestyle this would be for an opportunist. He would monitor their love lives to guard them from men who were there just for the money. No one foresaw the blooming of a love match between Briar and Thomas. It went on in the workshop in the shadows of the buildings. She was very happy and could not wait to get to work every morning, but no one guessed her underlying agenda. To Thomas's credit, he wasn't the one to make the first move, although he had fallen in love with her. He had fought his feelings for years and was resigned to the fact that to be in the same workspace as her was as far as it would go, as he respected her father and his job. The first move by Briar was when Thomas felt a hand on his butt, so he turned around only to find her standing close to him, waiting on his response. He started to walk away but she grabbed his arm and pulled him towards her.

"No, Briar this cannot happen. I'm much older than you and I respect your father," and it was at that moment she rested his hand on her breast. It was too much of a temptation for Thomas; his feelings took over. He had dreamt of this moment and now it was before him, he couldn't resist. He took Briar in his arms and held her tight. She pressed her body hard into his, arousing him, but guilt won out. "No, Briar, this must end here, it's not right," he said as he walked away. Briar begged him to stay but he continued walking, daring not to look back. He left the workshop to get some fresh air and reflect on what had just happened. He was meant to be the responsible one, the one to look up to, not someone who took advantage of the boss's daughter. He would make sure this never happened again, and much as he wanted her, she was out of bounds to him. He decided to go home early. Briar was disappointed with what had happened, but she was not about to give up. She felt he wanted her but today wasn't the right time. She would let it cool off for a while, but this would not be the end.

Willow

The wine harvesting was not long from beginning. Willow was right on to the sugar levels as these had to be tested regularly to determine ripeness. She had to let Alana know that the netting had to be pulled on today, as the birds were around in their droves. She had given Alana enough time to irrigate to ensure balanced growth, so now the grapes were in her capable hands. Willow had learnt at her viticultural course to sample grapes for the correct sugar level by using her palate, which was the best guide for the perfect harvest moment. She decided to give the grapes another week as the weather was to be hot so this would bring out the right sweetness. Because their vineyard covered so many acres, the grapes were going to be mechanically picked for efficiency. She had a small experimental block that she wanted picked by hand, for precision, just to compare the two methods to see if one had a better result than the other. She was looking for new ideas and ways to create a stand-out wine.

Willow went to the shed to talk with Thomas and Briar to see if the mechanical harvesters were ready to start next week. There were six harvesters lined up, all checked and ready to roll. "Who is going to operate them?" Willow asked.

"Thomas and I will operate one each. We will be the first harvesters until the full crop is ready to strip. How long before all the fruit has to come off?" asked Briar.

Willow said several acres on the sunny side of the rolling land facing the morning sun would be harvested first, then after another five days they could all be stripped.

"Thomas and I will tend to the first stripping, so hold off on employing anyone until they are needed. Will you tell Father, or do you want me to do it?" asked Briar.

"No, that's my job. I'm in charge of the harvesting," answered Willow.

Briar flicked Thomas a look and they both smiled, as here was Willow asserting her authority, letting them know what her position was. What they didn't understand was her deep knowledge of grapes and winemaking, which made her the creative heart of the vineyard.

Tonight, a pre- harvest party was being thrown, so all the permanent workers were invited to their boss's home for drinks and nibbles. They were regarded as part of the wider family, and this went down well with the staff as they felt important. Thomas and his wife were of course invited. Briar had never seen or met his wife, so she was looking forward to it. But she didn't know how she would feel, as all her feelings were focused on Thomas.

As they all started to arrive, in walked Thomas, all dressed up in a floral shirt and jeans. Briar had to slip into another room as she was besotted by him. She herself had taken extra care hoping Thomas would notice her, but his feelings started in the workshop while she was dressed in her overalls. It wasn't what she wore, it was her happy bubbly personality that attracted him, and her beautiful auburn hair that was always tucked under her hat; at times some would fall down around her shoulders, and this was when he found it hard not to go to her. He caught a glimpse of her before she left the room; when her long hair fell around her shoulders she was like an angel. Everyone was mixing and talk was rife. Thomas decided to move out on to the patio to have a moment to himself, only to find he was not alone. There standing further along on the patio was his angel. He wondered if he should go back inside, but the pull to her was too strong. He went over and rested his hand on her shoulder, fondling her beautiful hair.

Briar took his hand and led him through the garden and down the pathway then down to the workshop. Tonight, nothing was going to stop them, the game was on. She unzipped her dress and let it fall to the floor, leaving her standing in her bra and knickers. Thomas's willpower had gone, and his urges took over; down went his jeans and off came his shoes. He grabbed Briar and started kissing her body. She had never made love before and she felt tingles running through her body as she just stood there letting Thomas touch and kiss her. Her body started to ache as he caressed her breasts then moved his hands down her body. She whispered for him to take her. Just at that moment Thomas realised she may have never had sex before, so he abruptly stopped. "What's wrong?" she asked.

"Is this your first time?"

When Briar answered yes, he let her go.

"Please get dressed, I can't do this to you."

"But I want you, Thomas. I want you to be my first lover. Please teach me," she sobbed. It was all too much for him, the sobs, the pleas. He couldn't walk away now. He wanted to be gentle with her but they both got carried away, she wanted him right then, so it all happened, and he heard her squeal of delight.

"Thank you, Thomas, it was beautiful," she whispered, as he nestled his head in her auburn locks.

Briar left the workshop and headed back to the party, hoping she hadn't been missed.

"Where have you been, Briar?" asked her mother. "Thomas's wife wants to meet you. Come and I will introduce you."

"Not now, Mother. I have a stomach-ache. That's where I've been and now, I've got to go back, sorry," she said as she dashed off. How could she face his wife after what had just happened? Her party had finished, it was the best ever, just her and Thomas in the workshop together. She showered and went to bed knowing she was no longer a virgin, and proud that Thomas had stolen that from her.

Meanwhile Willow and Alana were enjoying themselves, trying different types of wine to see what they enjoyed most. The staff were having a great time as there were bottles of wine opened everywhere for them. Their father was watching the girls; he was proud of his daughters, and to think they all took trades that were relevant to the vineyard. Between them they had everything covered. Suddenly he noticed that Briar wasn't to be seen.

"Has anyone seen Briar?" he asked. Thomas was back joining in the party and when he heard that query he froze.

"It's alright dear, she has just gone to bed as she is not well," answered his wife.

When Thomas heard this, he felt relieved.

Harvesting had arrived

This was the much-awaited day, harvesting day, a significant milestone that they all looked forward to each year. The first two harvesters were driven by Thomas and Briar, as that was all that was needed for the first pick. The grapes had reached their peak ripeness to balance sugar, acid and tannin levels. When the grapes came in, they were sorted to remove unripe or damaged fruit as well as debris. Then the grapes were gently crushed to release their juice and remove the skins when making white wine. For red wines the skins were left in contact with the juice to extract colour and tannins. The harvesters started work from 4am so as to pick the grapes before it got too hot.

Now it was up to Willow to add the yeast extract, whether natural or cultured, to convert sugar into alcohol and carbon dioxide, as they were only making white wine this time. The fermentation temperatures varied at this stage, depending on the type of wine being made. White wines liked a cooler temperature, 10 to15°C, to preserve delicate aromas. Thomas and Briar's first day was over, and it was time to wash down the harvesters ready for the next day. Since the party night there had been many more love sessions in the workshop. They were now having a full-blown affair. Thomas was smitten with his beautiful young lover. She was willing and exciting. She had told him she had been to the doctor to go on the pill, but it had taken a fortnight to get the appointment, so they had unprotected sex during that time, not that Thomas knew this. Briar couldn't wait that long, not for a moment thinking that anything could happen: it was only two weeks!

Two weeks had passed and now all the harvesters were at work. The winery was a hive of activity, and Willow's excitement was growing. She worked alongside her father as he was the master winemaker, and she was learning all the time. At times she could see little things that could have been done differently, but as this year was her first vintage, she had to respect her father's ways. Next year things would change, as she had learnt more up-to-date techniques, but she didn't want to overshadow her father, which would be a mistake.

The winery itself was a magnificent building. Because there was family history dating back to King Henry I and owning a castle, the winery was constructed of stone. The outer walls consisted of long glass panels set between gabion baskets filled with stones that had come from the riverbed bordering their property.

The environment meant everything to the family, especially to Alana as the next generation. She wanted to preserve the creeks by planting alongside them. Her work with native plants symbolised her nurturing nature and her desire to create something lasting. Her projects connected the vineyard to the land's history and showed her respect for the environment. She also cared for the animals. The pigs in the walnut paddocks were under her care as she was always exploring the outskirts of the vineyard. Her vision was also the surrounding areas; they had to be cared for too.

Alana was the total opposite to Willow, whose ambitious intention was to produce that award-winning wine. But the efforts of both girls were needed to secure that dream. Alana knew this, but Willow was a little more focused on the end product, not for a moment thinking about the right soil acidities and sprays and the trellis systems that support the vines. The two girls got on reasonably well, although there were struggles at times to balance personal ambitions with their shared legacies.

The huge vats on the ground floor of the winery all shone like jewels as the sun peeped through the holes in the gabion baskets. On the second floor was the huge laboratory where all the experimenting was carried out, the accounts sections offices, a lovely big lounge, a kitchen then the management offices. The staff totalled seventy-five permanents and up to fifty casual workers which changed with each seasonal workload. This was a big operation and a successful one, and now with the next generation stepping up, it could only lead to more success.

It allowed their father to feel more at ease when doing his overseas promotions. This was his forte, he was a people person, and knew the biggest success was to keep the promotions ongoing. He was forever looking for new markets, and he attended many sales meetings. He believed in promoting his wines in New Zealand by discounting and putting glossy ads in popular magazines. His next flight was to America where he had already secured good outlets and a warehouse in the Napa Valley, where he had been doing trade for over four years. He was also lucky he had a good rapport with Ireland and the United Kingdom.

Briar, on the other hand, felt a little overshadowed at times because her mechanical work was less glamourous, but her personal life made up for any shortfalls. She had found love and was leading an exciting life right here in the workshop. Love happened at any time of the day just when the mood took them, as long as all the jobs were up to date, the harvesters ready when needed, keeping the grape crushing machines and sorting equipment working like clockwork. All three sisters were each as important as one another, otherwise the production line could not flow as smoothly as it did. Considering this was their first year as a team, all had gone well. The father was very proud of his daughters and he had kept a keen eye on them. Their lives were wholesome, just as he had planned. He knew any day the girls would be looking for partners, but he didn't want any opportunists hanging around them.

Alana had kept in touch with Timothy, the gardener at Epsom Girls Grammar. He rang often, asking questions about certain plants, which was also an excuse to talk with her. He liked her, as she was the only one who talked to him when he was new to the gardener's position. No one else seemed interested in the gardens, just Alana, so this was how their friendship began. He knew nothing of her background, and to him she was just another pupil at the college. He did know she lived in Blenheim, but that's as far as it went. He had contacted her because he had holidays due, and he wanted to meet up with her. It had been four years since he had last seen her. Perhaps they could visit some gardens. Alana told him she would like that, so they arranged a date and place to meet.

It was the girls' twenty-first birthday coming up in a week, and Alana's father had a surprise for her. He had arranged for a construction company to come to the vineyard and build a shade house and erect a large shed for Alana, so she could have her nursery to grow her plants and shrubs.. She had no idea this was about to happen; her sisters knew and were excited for her. This building process would be happening while she was away from the vineyard during the day, as she had asked for the week off to spend with Timothy. She definitely needed a safe place to store her pesticides and sprays under lock and key, as at the moment they were on a shelf in the workshop. The girls had their own vehicles so they could drive into Blenheim, which was 23 kilometres away, at any time.

Willow was in the winery every day working with the laboratory team. The huge stainless-steel vats preserved fresh, fruity profiles. These were commonly used for white and sparkling wines. The duration of the ageing ranged from a few months to several years, depending on the wine style. She had her own special vat with her trial grapes, the ones that were hand-picked instead of picked by the harvester. This was her pet project; she wanted to find out by treating the grapes differently whether it changed the taste of the wine. It was efficiency versus consistency, but was one to prove more palatable than the other?

Alana's visitor

THREE VAN LOADS of workers from the building company arrived to start work on Alana's nursery. She had left the vineyard as she was meeting Timothy at the local gardens. She didn't want him to know where she lived until she got to know him a little better. Alana remembered him telling her while at college that he had to find a job because he had to help his family with money. She thought perhaps they were a poor family who didn't have much, so she wanted to spend time with him to see if her feelings for him were real or imaginary. She enjoyed talking with him over the phone as they never ran out of conversation; was this because they shared interests?

As she had no idea about the new nursery, the family hoped she didn't come home before the workers left each day. As per their contract, the construction would be finished as promised by the end of the week. The family did ask that she bring Timothy home so they could meet him, especially her father as he wanted to see that he was worthy of his daughter.

Alana was seated in the café at the gardens, the arranged meeting place. She hadn't seen Timothy since her college days so didn't know what to expect. As she looked up, coming towards her was a tall pleasant-looking guy, but she didn't know if this was him, so she stayed seated. He walked up to her at the table. "Hi, Alana, did you not recognise me?" he asked. Poor Alana, she stood up and offered her hand, but he elected to give her a hug. This was not the shy boy weeding the gardens; he had certainly come out of his shell. Perhaps it was all those girls at the college.

"I'm sorry, Timothy, you're right, I didn't recognise you. You are a lot taller than I remember. Come and sit down so we can talk."

It didn't take long before they were engaged in conversation. Then it was time to go for a walk and test their plant knowledge, with perhaps a coffee and a bite to eat later. Alana was impressed with Timothy's naming of the plants, and it was obvious he had been studying his horticulture, so she commented on this.

"Yes, I have been studying, I'm currently sitting exams, but I can only do each module as I can afford it, as I'm also helping out my parents."

Alana asked what his parents did. He told her they had had a bad car accident ten years previously and neither had been able to work. His father was in a wheelchair and his mother used a walking stick for balance. There was just him and an older brother, but they weren't close, as he didn't offer to help with money. Tears came to her eyes; she couldn't imagine her parents being in this predicament. Here was a young man paying for his own education plus keeping his parents. She took a couple of minutes to reflect on her life; she never had to worry about paying for virtually anything, as there was always money available.

Alana wasn't sure how he travelled from Auckland to Blenheim, so she asked him.

"I flew to Wellington, came across on the ferry then caught a bus to here. I'm staying at a backpacker's hostel."

"How did you get here to the gardens?"

Timothy said he had walked there, and that he walked everywhere, which was why he was so tall. This made Alana laugh. She couldn't see the tie-up between walking and being tall. How he had changed from what she could remember, an adult now with a warm smile and a happy outlook on life. She did wonder how he just seemed to accept his life.

"Can I ask, are you happy with your life?" she asked.

"It's not what happens to you in life, it's how you deal with it that's important. My parents gave me a life for which I'm grateful, now it is my turn to repay them for that privilege."

With all her family's wealth, she had not heard such heartfelt emotions being expressed; it brought tears.

"Why the tears?" he asked. Alana reached for his hand and told him she had never met someone with such caring values.

"Tell me about your life. All I know is your name and

phone number, nothing else. Oh, yes, and you live in Blenheim."

This made her laugh; where would she start? She didn't want to frighten him off, so decided to go sparingly with her information. She told him she lived on a vineyard with her parents and two sisters.

"Are your sisters older than you?"

"No, we are the same age, but I am the youngest by one hour. We are triplets."

Timothy found this amusing, so they both laughed.

The afternoon flew by in the gardens enjoying each other's company, naming plants and trees with their botanical labels. As it was getting near teatime Timothy asked Alana if she would like to stay and have an evening meal with him. She agreed, so he suggested they walk back.

"No, we don't need to walk, I have a vehicle; we will drive there, that's if you trust me behind the wheel," she joked. The answer that came back shocked her.

"I'm far safer being driven by you, rather than the other way round, as I don't have a driver's licence, and I have never driven a car."

This floored Alana completely. What more shocks lay in store? How was he such a happy caring young man when he couldn't even drive?

"Is this your parents' vehicle?" he asked. She told him it was her own car and that the three sisters each had one. She asked him where he would like to go for a meal. He told her he was a stranger so asked her to lead the way.

Alana started to panic; did he have enough money to eat out? Where would she take him?

"I will take you to my favourite restaurant only if you let me pay."

Timothy wouldn't have a bar of it, as he had been working two jobs so he could afford this holiday and to take Alana for dinner. Alana suddenly did a backflip and changed eating places: she would take him to one that had a big menu and was less expensive.

While they were waiting for their meals, Timothy asked Alana if she would like a drink. Yes, she would like a Pinot Noir. He didn't know what this drink was.

"Is that the name I ask for at the bar?" He came back with a beer and a glass of red wine. "Have you ever tried a wine?" she asked.

"Not really, I haven't had an occasion to drink wine, but one day I will try it as this seems to be what people are drinking today. My parents could never afford to buy alcohol, so it was never part of my life." Alana felt sad; it was as if she was talking to someone from a Third World country.

She couldn't help herself, she just had to ask, "Timothy, to me your life sounds quite sad, but you always seem to be happy; how can that be?"

"I have learnt that first of all comes love and respect, then I set myself personal goals and work hard hoping they come true. But all the time not forgetting how I came to be here, so I help my parents out with money. I read this article that never leaves my head, and it goes

'Everyone should at least once in a lifetime turn a dream into reality'. I'm working on this."

All the time while listening to Timothy, she realised how far apart their lives were, but she had never met such a humble and caring person. She felt she just wanted to hold him and reassure him that everything was going to be okay. She felt humbled herself for having met someone with very little, but who treasured life for whatever it was. This day she would remember forever.

When they left the restaurant, Alana said she would drop him off at his lodgings. As they pulled up in front of the backpackers, she switched the ignition off. She felt a new world had open up before her, one she had no insight into. She wanted to hold his hand and thank him for the person he was. But before she started, Timothy was thanking her, saying, "What lovely company you are. Can we meet again tomorrow?"

That night when she pulled up at her home, she sat in the car thinking about the day. It hadn't cost very much, yet it was the most rewarding day she could remember having. He proved that one didn't have to have much money or glamourous things or even a driver's licence to appreciate life. How bloody moving was that? Her family were waiting inside to see how her date went. She burst into tears; where would she start? She relayed her day to them, and like her, they were humbled. Did people really live like that? How do they move on from these situations? But not to have a driver's licence or even have driven a car, what future did he have, now that he was an adult? "You won't want to be seeing him again," said the father. Alana excused herself, as she need time to herself and think over the day.

How could she give up on him? He had stirred feelings in her body that she never knew were there; besides, she had agreed to spend the next day with him. Something had changed Alana, and she could not understand how having so little, one could still be happy and have a mindset that made others envious of 'that poor person'. Then she remembered a caption she once read: 'A person with very little is not poor, a poor person is someone with everything but wants more.' Her privileged life seemed unimportant. Timothy had lived his life not focused on himself but rather on those that needed him.

As Alana was driving to the backpackers to pick up Timothy, she stopped off at a sandwich bar and bought two picnic lunches. She thought it would be nice just the two of them together, away from it all. This would give her a chance to work out why he was the person he was, so selfless and caring, especially when he had very few material assets. She decided they would drive to Waikawa where they could sit and watch the yachts and launches coming and going, perhaps then she could fathom him out and understand who he was. He was a mystery.

As she pulled up outside the backpackers, there he was waiting for her. He came over to the car and jumped in, greeting her. "Hi, Alana, I'm looking forward to today. What are we going to do?" She told him it was a surprise.

"A surprise will be wonderful; I don't have many of them."

Alana thought to herself, she could surprise him plenty

if she revealed her life, but this was not about her, this was about him.

"What did you do last night when I dropped you off?" He told her did some study as he had exams coming up.

"You actually brought your work with you on a holiday?"

"I have to keep learning as I want good marks, and you can only achieve that if they keep at it. I want to make something of my life, I have dreams, and they can only work if I keep on to them. They don't just happen by themselves, my dreams anyway.

"What are your dreams, Timothy? Am I allowed to ask?"

"Not at the moment while you are driving; you might run us off the road," he chuckled. This made Alana laugh. He was a delight to be around, as he turned every situation into happy moments. This, she felt, was a gift.

As they drove up to the marina, Timothy couldn't help himself. "Look at all that wealth. I wonder if they are happy owning such luxury. Can we go for a walk down the piers and see if we can meet someone who owns one of these?"

Alana told him today was his and they would do what he wanted.

"No, today is ours, and we will do things together."

They made their way down to a pier to see if they could see life anywhere. Timothy spotted a man working on a mast, so that was the direction they were heading. When they got near, he called out to the man, "Lovely day," and the answer they got back was "It would be okay if this bloody mast didn't have to be repaired."

"But apart from that all must be good," asked Timothy.

"Don't own a boat: they cost money all the way, and take up unnecessary time," the man replied.

As they carried on walking, Timothy took Alana's hand. "See, I've proved a point: all the money in the world doesn't make for happiness. I bet he would rather be us walking along the pier holding hands with not a worry in the world."

"You are so right, Timothy. What makes you a happy person? I can't understand why you always see the bright side of life, even when it's dull.

"If I haven't learnt why life is so precious by now, then I wouldn't be the person I am today. I have seen a lot of sadness, especially in my own family, and it has taught me to fully appreciate every moment of every day."

The more time Alana spent with Timothy the more drawn to him she felt. He was such a positive person. Of all the people she knew, no one had such love for life as him, yet he would own less than anyone she knew.

Timothy was getting peckish so suggested they find somewhere to go for lunch. Alana told him that was taken care of and went to the car boot and brought out the picnic boxes. They sat in the car away from the pesky seagulls who were hovering around looking for any leftovers.

"Are you an organised person, Alana?" he asked.

"I guess I would have to say yes; why do you ask?"

"Just curious."

By the end of the day, she had worked out what made Timothy tick. Now she was worried when he found out about her life that it might be a turn-off. He didn't mix where there was wealth, that was shown when he saw all the yachts and cruisers. She never wanted him to think he was less of a being than her, because this wasn't true. In her mind he was the better person; his values far outweighed hers. Over the next few days, they did things together and enjoyed each other's company.

Alana asked Timothy to come to her twenty-first birthday party the next night, saying she would pick him up in the afternoon and bring him out to their winery where he could stay the night, so she wouldn't have to drive him home in the dark. He protested that he didn't have any flash clothes for a party. She told him not to worry, just for him to be there was the most important thing. She also said no presents were to be bought, as she didn't fully know his financial situation.

Party night had arrived; family friends were invited as was Thomas and his wife along with other permanent staff. Alana knew that Timothy was going to be thought of as a misfit, but she didn't care, because of all the people she wanted to be with tonight, it was with him. Since being in his company, she could see what was valued most in life, and that was life itself. It was something money couldn't buy; it was a deep acceptance of who you are and being able to laugh and find humour. Most of the time Alana's family lived a rushed life as there were always things to do.

Alana was on her way home to the vineyard with

Timothy. He had never seen so many acres planted in grapes, and he noticed the homes were very grand. In his mind she lived on a vineyard, full stop, but his thinking never went beyond that. When they reached the start of a property, he noticed a sign saying not to enter without permission. "Do you have permission?" he asked. She pulled off the road and turned the ignition off.

"I didn't tell you, Timothy, because I thought you wouldn't like me, but all the land you see ahead is my family's vineyard."

"Wow, this takes me straight back to the marina with all the expensive toys. What is that huge building over there?"

"That is our winery where all our wine is made. Please don't dislike me for not telling you about my life," she begged. Silence reigned while Alana kept driving, and because the land was undulating the drive seemed endless. As the home came into view, Timothy said, "Blimey heck, I'm flabbergasted Alana. I thought you were an average girl with an education, but look at all this." He was in disbelief. Never had he been where there was so much wealth. As she pulled into the driveway, there to meet them was her family.

"Don't feel afraid, I'm by your side. I respect you for who you are Timothy. We are no better than you, and in fact your values would outshine us all."

He didn't know where to look; it all seemed too much. Alana opened the car door and took his hand and led him to meet the family. "Hi, everyone, this is Timothy." They all looked at him. He was certainly different to most visitors that came here to their vineyard.

"Hi everyone, I'm pleased to meet you all. A little surprised though, I must say." This remark brought smiles to their faces.

"I hadn't told Timothy about my life, so he knew very little about the vineyard. No wonder he is surprised."

Alana's father came forward and shook his hand.

"Welcome to our patch, Timothy", then everyone introduced themselves.

"Before we settle in, I have a surprise for you, Alana. Jump into your car with Timothy and follow us."

They drove for a further couple of kilometres, all the time still on their property. When they stopped, there before them was a huge shade house and another large building. Alana couldn't believe her eyes as she pulled up. She jumped out of the car and ran to her father.

"Happy birthday, daughter, this is your birthday present." Everyone clapped and cheered. By this time Timothy had got out of the car and joined everyone. He couldn't believe what he had just witnessed; who would get all this for a birthday present? He thought this was so extravagant. How did he get himself involved in such wealth? He felt uneasy. Alana sensed he was overcome so took his arm and led him into the shade house.

"This is what Alana wanted, to have her own nursery to grow all the plants needed to keep our waterways pristine. Now that you have it, my dear, I hope you are happy," announced her father.

At that moment nothing could have been further from

her mind. Why did this have to happen right now? It was a lovely surprise, but it came at an inappropriate time. She knew what Timothy would be thinking, that he didn't belong here. She thanked her father and said she and Timothy would stay on for a while, and they would see everyone back home. Everyone left. There alone stood Alana and Timothy. She could see the look of disbelief on his face.

"I'm sorry, Timothy, this must have been a shock for you. What are you thinking?"

He hesitated. "Who gets a shade house and a building for a birthday present? I still can't get my head around it. This would be my life's dream, a goal to work towards, but a birthday present! I'm blown away; this is a totally different world to where I belong."

"Please don't say that. I know our worlds are opposites, but I like you. Your values are way above mine and that's what I like most about you, it's not what you're got, it's who you are." Alana felt for Timothy and she could understand it was a shock for him to see all this extravagance. They were silent a while.

"I haven't got much apart from my values," said Timothy finally, "but I am happy with who I am. I have never put a price on material possessions as I don't have any."

Alana put her arms around him, hoping he would feel wanted.

"You are a lovely person, Timothy, and I'm proud to have met you. I have learnt so much from you. Come and have a look around with me. I'm happy as now I have somewhere to grow my seedlings, and I do worry about the manures and sprays, as now they are not stored properly, so I will block off a bay at the end where I can keep them under lock and key. Shall we head home now? Are you happy to go back?"

At this point, he was not comfortable with anything, as this was a world way beyond his means.

Alana showed Timothy to his room. This just added to the sense of wealth that surrounded him since his arrival. She told him her bedroom was next door so when he was ready, to come and knock on her door. The look on his face let Alana know that he needed down time, as she noticed his smile was not his natural one. She worried about this night and whether it would be too overwhelming for him. She didn't want their friendship to end at this early stage.

An hour had passed when she heard the knock so she asked him to come and sit on her bed so they could talk. An awkward silent moment passed, and it was Alana who spoke first.

"I know this is a lot for you to take in, but underneath we are just ordinary people. Please don't judge me by what you have seen. All these are material things; they aren't us."

Timothy looked her straight in the eye. "Alana, I don't think our friendship is going to work. I could never give you the life you are accustomed to. All I can offer is love and respect, but that will never be enough, as I never imagined this to be your life. You didn't fit the picture I had in my mind. I knew you were well educated, but this is all too much."

She asked him to accompany her on a walk to the winery, so he could see things for himself and then perhaps understand a little more about her life. As they walked through the vineyard without talking, she took his hand. Once they reached the huge building the first thing he noticed were the stone walls, made up of gabion baskets and glass panels from the bottom to the top, making the structure look like a work of art. There were birds fluttering everywhere as they were making nests between the stones in the baskets. As they walked through the door, he was dazzled by the sheer size of the building and the rows and rows of big shiny tanks. He had to know all about these and Alana was only too willing to explain.

"The vats are full of wine that we have made from this year's harvest. Come on up the stairs and see where the laboratory and offices are."

"Why do you need a laboratory?"

There were people milling around everywhere carrying out their allocated jobs. She explained there were lots of techniques to producing a good wine.

"This is where all the experimenting is carried out. My sister Willow is a qualified winemaker so this will be her department one day."

Timothy looked down at all the vats. He had never seen anything like this before; everything was spotless.

"I'm more interested in conservation, so all the planting of native shrubs by the streams I have helped with. We used to buy in all the vegetation we needed, but it will work out much cheaper if we can grow everything on our own property. The sprays and soil testing are also my domain, as is the irrigating and the pigs." Timothy didn't associate Alana with pigs; this brought a smile. She could see he was a little more relaxed. Had she done enough to change his mind?

Instead of cooking dinner the family decided to have drinks and an array of nibbles which would be ongoing until the party ended. Friends and staff were arriving, so Alana was needed to serve drinks for the guests. She told Timothy she would come and get him when her duties were finished, otherwise he would feel uncomfortable being left on his own.

The bar was covered with open bottles of all varieties of their wine, sparking, stills and reds. This was a three-way celebration, three twenty-firsts together, so of course the girls were the 'celebrities' of the night. Once everyone had a glass in their hand, Alana went to get Timothy. He was feeling he was an outsider, but he wouldn't let Alana down on this special night. She looked beautiful.

"You look stunning tonight, Alana, I feel proud to be your partner this evening. I'm not as stylish as you, but my heart is in the right place, so that makes me happy. As you know material things don't matter to me, probably because they have never been part of my modest life. I have brought you a little gift, so I hope you like it."

As she opened it, in a box lay a beautiful silver-plated 'Alana' dress pin. She was so happy she asked Timothy to pin it on her. He told her she didn't have to wear it tonight. "But I love it, Timothy. Every time I wear it, I will think of you. This is so special, thank you," and she kissed his cheek.

Together they went down to meet the guests. He had never seen so much glamour and he had to admit to himself it was lovely to be part of, even if it was the only time this happened in his lifetime. To see the bar covered with so many opened bottles of wine was mindboggling. Alana's father came up to them and kissed his daughter, then asked Timothy what wine he would like to drink.

"I've never tasted wine, so I don't know," he announced. Her father stood in disbelief. This person had never tasted wine. This was a first; where had Timothy been all his life? He certainly didn't fit into this family!

"It's okay, Father, I'll get Timothy a drink," interrupted Alana. She asked him if he would prefer to try a sweet, medium, or a slightly dry wine. Poor Timothy he was out of his depth. He told her to pick a nice one. While she was away getting his drink, Briar came over to talk to him. She wore a dressy bib overall outfit.

"I'm a mechanic as you can see by my outfit. It is styled on my work overalls, only made of nicer fabric. Give me tractors any day or any type of machinery and I'm in my element. Thomas, who I work with, and I look after all the machinery, harvesters and vehicles on the place. What do you work at?"

Timothy told her he was studying, in fact sitting exams in horticulture, as soon as got back to Auckland.

"Oh well, you and Alana will be well suited, as she loves seedling and plants. That's why Father built her her own nursery so she can grow all the plants for the vineyard. Here is Alana coming back … nice to talk with you," and with this she moved away.

He had felt at ease with Briar; she seemed to be a down-to-earth type of girl. Alana arrived back with a glass of Pinot Gris for Timothy to try. She watched as he took his first sip, his nose twitched, and he coughed, the sip was too big and it caught him unawares. He wasn't used to this taste; it was certainly different to anything he had tried. He wasn't sure what he thought of it so put on a brave face. Perhaps his perception of the wealthy needed to be reassessed, although in her father's company he felt uncomfortable, as if he wasn't accepted as a suitable partner for his daughter.

An announcement was made for the girls to come up to the bar, so everybody could sing to them, and they together would cut the cake. Before them stood the girls, all totally different, Willow being the standout; she oozed fashion. Briar was the tomboy and Alana, who Timothy thought was lovely, was perhaps the least good-looking one. Neither of Alana's sisters had a partner. The girls blew out the candles and everyone sang the birthday song.

As the night was drawing to a close, Willow came up to Timothy and made herself known. He told her he was most impressed with the winery; it was the first time he had visited one.

"Oh, so you don't socialise at wineries?" she asked.

"No, I'm just an ordinary type of guy. I work during the day and come home and cook dinner for my parents at night, then I study."

"Wow, you would be a good catch, perhaps I should steal you," she said jokingly.

"I only have eyes for Alana," he answered, not quite seeing the funny side.

"I will get you another wine. Yours is empty," and she took his glass and came back with a new one. Meanwhile Alana had gone to the bathroom.

"Here you are, Timothy, this one is our most expensive wines." He thanked Willow but she didn't have to give him the most expensive wine. He took one sip and, yes, it did taste nicer than the one he had, but that might because his palate was getting used to wines. Perhaps price defined the wine! He would keep that on the backburner; was he learning something about wines? He was only halfway through his drink when the guests started leaving, he would have to finish it quickly, so they could get cleaned up. But this was a bad decision as he nearly choked, and the wine burned as it made its way down his throat. Alana came rushing over to see if he was okay, but all he could do was signal that he was fine. She took his glass and said she would be back in a moment with a glass of water. After swallowing some water, the coughing stopped, and all seemed normal again.

"I'm sorry if I caused you any embarrassment. I will remember next time I have wine just to sip it, not gulp it." Alana assured him she wasn't embarrassed. Timothy asked her if it was alright for him to go to his room now that everybody had left.

"Yes, that's fine. I will stay behind and help clean up.

Did you enjoy yourself or did you suffer? Give me an honest opinion."

"I did enjoy myself, although I felt out of my comfort zone at times, but that is my problem not anyone else's. I'm not used to such luxury. But it is nice to experience the difference between my life and yours. If I had known at the start this was your life, then I probably would not have kept in touch with you."

This shocked Alana; she could see he was belittling himself, so she needed to give him a boost.

"I would have been terribly disappointed if you gave up on me because of who I am. We are both equals; it is just that we have come from different backgrounds, but that shouldn't interfere with our relationship. We are two people who like each other and that is all that matters, and backgrounds are irrelevant."

Timothy was surprised that was the way she thought; it made him think that he had to change the way he thought about himself. He thanked her for a nice night and said he would see her in the morning.

As they all sat round the breakfast table the next morning, Alana was next to Timothy, so he didn't feel isolated. Her mother was the first to ask him a question.

"Did you fly down or drive down?" He told her he flew down because he didn't have a driver's licence. Then she wanted to know how he got around, and he told her he either walked or cycled.

"My parents had a car, but it was written off when they had their accident, and because of their injuries they never bothered to replace it. One day I hope to buy my own car, but at the moment I am helping to keep my parents, they are my main concern."

"That's nice to hear, Timothy," said the mother. Then the father spoke; he had to find out more. "What is your ambition in life?"

Timothy though for a moment. "I am studying to become a horticulturist. I do extra exam papers as I can afford them, so it is taking me longer than the average person to complete the course, I am determined so I know I will get there."

"Good on you lad, that's the spirit, that's what I like to hear. Everyone needs a goal to work to, otherwise you waste precious time."

When they had finished breakfast, Timothy thanked the family for having him as a guest.

"I have learnt so much from this visit; it has opened my eyes as to how big the outside picture is, so thank you all."

Now it was time to take Timothy back to the backpacker's accommodation, as the next day he was flying back to Auckland. Alana knew she would miss him as he was the most wholesome person she had met. As they pulled up at the hostel, Alana said, "I hope you can come again, but next time stay with us. I'm truly going to miss you, you are a lovely person, and I want you to know I have feelings for you Timothy. I don't know if they are reciprocal?" Before she could finish, he reached for her hand, and said to her, "Your words have made me very happy as I feel the same. I still see that barrier of wealth and I wonder in the end if this will divide us. But let us enjoy the rest of the day together."

Alana had a brainwave. "Why don't you book out of here and I will drive you to Picton? You could spend the night there and just walk to the ferry in the morning. That will save you having to get up early and catch the bus from Blenheim, then have to wait in Picton." Timothy thought on this, but it meant driving back on her own, so he mentioned this to her.

"I've driven this road many times and it is like second nature to me, so please let me do this for you."

Timothy let go of her hand and leant over and kissed her cheek. He said he would check out and pay then be right back. Alana was happy he accepted her offer as it gave them more time together.

As they entered Picton they noticed the 'no vacancy' sign up on all the accommodation places, and this was also the case at the backpackers. This worried Timothy as he didn't have enough money to cover a night in an expensive place and all the cheaper motels were full. Alana could see panic starting to set in, so drove around to the marina where there were vacancies at the more expensive motels. She went into the hotel and asked if they had a vacancy for the night. She was asked how many people it was for, and she let them know there would be one but possibly two. The receptionist quoted a price that would cover two people, so she paid and picked up the key. She went back out to the car.

"Right, Timothy, you are staying here for the night, it is all paid for, and I don't want you to protest. All you have to do tomorrow is walk across the overhead bridge to the ferry terminal. I'll come with you and unlock the door while you bring your belongings."

As they walked into the room, there to greet them was a lovely harbour view.

"This is lovely, Alana, thank you. Please stay a while. We will get takeaways for tea, then we can sit and enjoy the view."

At 6pm they went for a walk to find a takeaway shop; they ordered then brought it back to the unit to eat. Conversation between the two of them flowed easily and before they realised, darkness had set in.

Timothy said,

"You can't drive home in the dark. Besides, it is getting late. Stay the night and drive home in the morning."

Alana agreed as the night had got away on them. When it was time to bunk down, there was only a queen bed in the bedroom so Timothy offered for Alana to sleep in the bed, and he would sleep on the settee.

"No, we will share the bed; that is only fair," she said.

When they climbed into bed Timothy put the spare pillows between them, but it wasn't long before they were removed. Alana was the instigator as she rolled over and cuddled into him. Then they began kissing and getting their bodies close to each other. It was Timothy that broke the silence. "As much as I would like to make love, I don't think we have known each other long enough. It's not that I don't want to, very much so, but I have principles to which I live by. I would never want you to regret anything we had done together if this relationship didn't work out."

Alana was surprised, but she admired him for what he

stood for. They cuddled up together and she felt safe in his arms.

The next morning when they awoke, they looked at each other and laughed. Although they slept together, they were both still virgins. Alana was happy that Timothy took the stand he did, as there was no embarrassment for either of them, and now there was something to look forward to in the future. They made their way to a café and had breakfast then it was time to say goodbye as Timothy had to check in at the ferry terminal. It was a sad parting but they both knew they would keep in touch. This was now more than just a conversation between two people over the phone; it had advanced to the next stage. Alana held on to him as they kissed goodbye then she whispered, "Please don't go home and think my life is so different to yours. We have the same feelings, we are just two people who like each other. Bye, Timothy, have a safe journey."

After seeing Timothy off, Alana left Picton and drove home to the vineyard, all the way thinking about him and his values in life. He may be poor, but his heart was in the right place, and she loved him for all the right reasons, hoping her background wasn't going to be a hindrance to their friendship. This was one time when she wished her life wasn't so different, and that things didn't come so easy, because Timothy was living proof of a person who took nothing for granted and enjoyed every moment that was available to him. He had experienced hardships and through these he had learnt that life can be rewarding without the comforts of money. This was a privilege that had to be earned, not bought. Would the different lifestyles be a dividing factor in this relationship? Alana hoped this would not be so.

The distance between them was going to be hard to manage, but now their feelings were out in the open, hopefully they would continue to express these to each other.

The family were all gathered for lunch when Alana arrived home. Her father asked her why she hadn't come home the previous night, so she explained how she took Timothy to Picton so he didn't have to catch an early bus the next morning. They talked and had takeaways, and before they realised it was dark, so he didn't want her to drive home alone.

"I stayed in the unit with Timothy. He slept on the settee, and I had the bed," she explained. Not quite the truth but nothing happened so no other details were required. She asked, "What did you think of Timothy?"

"He seems a decent young lad, but surely you are not serious about him. He has nothing to offer, not even a driver's licence. There are plenty of other young men out there that would have more to offer," replied her father. Alana was hurt by her father's response. Timothy couldn't help where he came from, he was making his own way in life to better himself, but rather than argue she just left things as they were. Background meant very little to her; respect and caring came first, and Timothy had these qualities.

Feeling hurt, Alana left the house and went to the garden shed and loaded some of her seedlings and cuttings into the boot of her car and drove to her new nursery. She was excited to have this place of her own, but it was only now she could think how lucky she was. She had had different feelings when all was exposed in front of Timothy. He was not used to such extravagance, but to Alana it was just life.

She felt this was a new beginning for her. Her plants were at different stages of growth, so now she had room to spread them out into their separate areas. She could see she had a lot of work ahead, but this was the challenge she needed. Also, because she was now closer to the pig run, she would bring the bags of food up and store them in her shed.

Briar takes time out

Now that this year's harvest was over and it was a quieter time for Thomas and Briar in the workshop, there was no pressure to have the machinery ready and waiting to be used. It was the yearly maintenance on the tractors and vehicles for the next couple of months, plus Thomas took his holidays at this time of the year, leaving Briar to run the workshop. Their affair was still going strong, so Thomas wasn't looking forward to being away from Briar for two weeks, but as his holidays were due, they had to be taken.

While in the workshop on her own, Briar noticed it was getting a little difficult to bend over; was this due to the weight gain she was noticing? She decided to cut back on her eating so asked the family not to dish her such big meals. The family had noticed this too, so went along with her decisions. Luckily, with Thomas away, if she felt exhausted, she could sit down and rest. But this was causing her some worry, so next time she was in town she went to the medical centre to make a doctor's appointment. There was an appointment available within the next half hour, and she decided to wait.

After explaining her problem to the doctor, he asked her if she was in a relationship, to which she answered no. After a lot of questions, he decided to do a pregnancy test, which came back positive. This was a huge shock to Briar, so then she had to explain that she was in a casual relationship. The doctor did an ultrasound examination to see how far along she was, only to find she was between four and five months, so an abortion was not an option; she would have to carry the baby to full term.

Here before her were the cold hard facts of life, something she had never encountered. Briar's mind was ablaze with questions: what would she do? She couldn't let it be known that it was Thomas's baby, as that would bring shame, and her father would sack him on the spot. This would probably make him want to shift away and she wouldn't see him again, which would break her heart. She had to think of a way to handle this on her own; her parents must not know. Thank goodness Thomas was on holiday, as this way she didn't have to face him, and when he returned to work it was her time to take her annual leave. She would have to think of something within the next two weeks.

Briar's mind couldn't rest; she was trying to work out how she could be absent for four months without anyone knowing why! She would miss Thomas most of all, but she couldn't risk him losing his position as their head mechanic. After many hours of soul-searching, she was putting a plan in place. She didn't know yet how she was going to ask for four months' leave, but she had decided she would keep the baby and hire a live-in nanny. She would rent a flat, and that way she would be a hands-on mum. She could never imagine giving up Thomas's baby as it was conceived out of pure love. This would be his first child, but at this stage she didn't know if she would ever tell him.

The first step was to break the news to her family that she was going to go flatting, as she wanted her independence. They were not happy to be losing one of their daughters, but she was of age to make her own decisions. Her father pointed out she had to factor in the cost of fuel to come and go each day as well as pay rent. She knew it was going to be tough, but there was no alternative if she wanted to keep the baby. Their grandfather had left the three girls an inheritance, of which they could access once they turned twenty-one. In the family there was an inheritance to be passed down to the eldest child of each generation, but because they were triplets it was shared among them. The first child in the next generation would receive an inheritance, this was a right for each generation.

If things became too tough, she could use her inheritance to help her through. There was another alternative: she could use the inheritance as a substantial deposit on buying her own home, and instead of paying rent she would be paying off a mortgage. She talked this over with her father and he agreed, as why pay rent when one could be paying off their own mortgage? He was a sound businessman and this was the logical thing to do.

For the next week Briar and her father attended several house auctions and were lucky enough to put forward the highest bid on a home she really liked, so now she was the proud owner of her own home. The agent would give her the keys as soon as the deposit was paid as he knew the family. There would be no problems there, as they were known as a wealthy family.

Briar received the keys to her own home. She had been to a second-hand shop and bought all that she needed to start with, as she knew there were many expenses to come. She decided to tread carefully and have money in reserve. This is where her budgeting would begin. Only one big question was left: how was she going to ask for four months off? She would have to leave the area and go where no one knew her, or any family members.

It did not sit well with Briar having to tell her family untruths, but she had no other choice. This was the night to ask her father if she could take four months' leave.

"Father, my friend and her mother had booked to go to the UK and they were meant to leave this week, but in the meantime her mother was involved in a motor accident and is not allowed to travel, so she has asked me if I would take her mother's place, as she is too frightened to travel on her own. The fares are paid for, so I don't have to worry about them; they just want me to go to keep her company. They have booked for four months, but I would be back at the start of next season's harvest. It would just mean Thomas would have to do the servicing of the vehicles, but it is our quieter time."

Her father had to think on this, as she had just purchased a home and there would be no wages coming in, so how was she going to make the mortgage payments?

"I'll rent it out for the four months. There are always people wanting short-term rentals. I'll speak to the agent tomorrow."

Her father liked that she was using her head to cover her house payments while she was away.

"Briar, this is a good chance for you to see some of the world, so, yes, we will manage until you come home."

She thanked her father, but deep down in her heart she was hurting. This was the second secret she had kept from the family. First the affair with Thomas and now her pregnancy. She was not happy with herself as she felt she was letting the family down, not that they had any idea what was going on in her life.

Today Thomas was returning to work after taking his annual leave. He couldn't wait to see Briar and take her in his arms, as he had dreamt of this moment right from the first day away from the vineyard. Now that he was back, resuming their affair was only minutes away, and he could hardly wait. As he entered the workshop, there she was, her hair hung loose today, not tucked under her hat, so he made a beeline straight for her and wrapped his arms around her, resting his head in her beautiful hair.

"I'm back, my darling, I've missed you so much, the time stood still while I was away, the days couldn't pass quick enough, now here we are together again."

Briar turned around and clung to Thomas; she couldn't hide the tears that trickled down her face. Were they tears of joy or tears of heartbreak, as now she had to tell him she was leaving the next day and would be gone for four months.

"Why the tears, Briar?"

She sobbed as she told him this was her last day at work for four months.

"Oh my God, two weeks seemed like a lifetime. How will I last four months? I will miss you so much Briar, promise me you will stay true to me. No, I can't ask you to do that, you are young and free. I will be waiting for you when you come home. Ring me often and let me know you are safe."

Briar desperately wanted to tell him she would be true to him because she was carrying his baby, so there would be no one else, but this had to remain her secret. She told Thomas she had bought a home and had moved out of the vineyard. So much had happened during his absence from the workshop, he felt everything was falling apart.

"Did you fall out with your family?" he asked. Briar reassured him she moved out because she wanted her independence. No, she loved her family, but she just needed some breathing space. Thomas heard a vehicle, so that was a warning that someone was arriving, and he let Briar go and they both started back to work.

"Hi, Thomas, did you have a good break?' asked Briar's father.

"Yes, boss, but it is always good to get back to work

again. I prefer work to holidaying, to me it just seems a waste of time really."

"Well, it's good to hear you are happy to be back. It makes for a good work relationship," he replied. He continued with his business as did Thomas and Briar.

When the workshop was free of workers, it was time for Thomas and Briar to make up for lost time, and for a future that had to be put on hold. This was their last love-making session before their baby was born, so Briar went all out to make sure she would remember this afternoon forever. Thomas was amazed at her enthusiasm, that's why he loved her,: she was full of energy and surprises. He even shed tears knowing tomorrow she would be gone. The workshop would not be the same without her, but he could always fall back on the many memories they shared in this very space.

The agent who sold Briar her home had a tenant wanting a short-term rental, so she left it to him to handle while she was away. Sad goodbyes were said by all family members, but none sadder than Briar who was living a life of untruths. She never set out to live a life of deception, but one thing led to another, resulting in her falling pregnant and having to face the consequences alone. It was not going to be an easy ride, and she accepted that there had to be consequences for her actions, and the result was she could never part with Thomas's baby.

Secretly, she had contacted a girlfriend from her college days and explained her predicament. Her friend knew of a position coming up, that of a live-in position for a house and pet sitter while the owners went on sabbatical leave. Briar asked if she could meet the people, but her friend said they were desperate for someone as they had to leave within the next week, so she would recommend Briar, and they would take it from there. The following day her friend reported to her, and the job was hers. This would be where she would spend her next four months. No money was to exchange hands for rent; this was covered by the minding of the home and the pets.

Time passes by

THREE MONTHS HAD PASSED without any hiccups, and Briar was grateful that no one was suffering because of her situation. On the days she felt tired she would just rest, and her thoughts would drift back to Thomas, then the tears would start. Each day she made sure she took the dog for a walk on its leash as she didn't want it to run away. The cat was not a worry as it just came and went as it pleased.

She rang the family and gave them false information, and beforehand she had to study up on the areas she was meant to be in, so if questions were asked, she was covered. She couldn't send postcards as was requested by the family; that was totally out of the question. Each phone call was kept short as she always pointed out that it was costly to call from the UK. She had called Thomas three times during work hours; he was easy to talk to as he didn't ask questions and just wanted to hear that she still loved him, as he did her.

Time was running out for Briar as there were just two more weeks before the owners returned from their sabbatical. Her midwife had told her it would be any day now as the baby was ready to come. As soon as her waters broke, she had to call her, and she would come and pick her up and take her to the maternity home. This was when Briar started to feel alone, and not having the blessing of her family made her sad. But then as her thoughts switched to Thomas, the sadness disappeared and a warm feeling embraced her, and this gave her the strength to carry on.

The time had arrived, and Briar started in labour. Her midwife stayed with her to help her cope with the pain. Several hours passed and she felt she was being punished for her sins, but this was all part of having a baby; it didn't come easy. Six hours later she gave birth to a baby boy. This was the first male to be born in two generations. Sadly, would his birth ever be acknowledged? Would that privilege be denied to him?

The midwife had a friend who was a nanny and who had just returned from overseas and was looking for a live-in position. She was in her early thirties and had nursing training. The two met and an immediate feeling of relief hit Briar, for here was the answer to her prayers. For the first couple of days baby was not coping with breastfeeding, so the nurse put together a formula as a standby. Briar was not allowed to leave the maternity home until the feeding situation was sorted. This took another two days, but this was good for her as she could catch up on some much-needed rest.

A bond was starting to form between mother and son. It didn't happen immediately, but as Briar held her baby she thought of her wonderful times with Thomas, and this cemented everything. This little bundle of joy was born out of love, so how could he not be loved?

Briar called her real-estate agent to see if her home was still being rented. It was, but the tenants were moving out at the weekend. She asked him to get cleaners in after they had left, so it would be ready for her when she went home, perhaps on Wednesday, depending on flights. Before they left, Briar had to explain her situation to the nanny to avoid any confusion. The nanny took it all on board and thought Briar was a level-headed young person, having gone through all this on her own. The next job was to name baby, but she had already thought on this and decided on Thomas's middle name … so baby James it was.

Briar managed to get flights for them, so they flew from Auckland to Wellington then caught a connecting flight to Blenheim. She hadn't told the family she was on her way home as she wanted time to settle in, and there would be a barrage of questions that she would have to answer. They caught a taxi from the airport to her home and managed to get James settled without too much fuss. Briar only had the bare essentials for the baby, so tomorrow she would have to do some shopping. But first she and the nanny would have to sit and talk about how they were going to explain the baby to her family.

They decided that James was going to be passed off as the nanny's baby and they were boarding with Briar. This way she could still be a hands-on mum without her family knowing the truth. Once settled, she would introduce the nanny and James to her family and to Thomas. She couldn't wait to be back at work with Thomas. This year's harvest was just beginning so their workload was about to begin. Briar had worked hard at getting her body back into shape, and although she was still carrying a little extra weight, this was easily explained as too much food consumed while on holiday. Once she was back at work it would soon fall off.

Today Briar made her way to the vineyard, and first she wanted to call in on Thomas and then she would have to face the family.. As yet no one knew she was home, so it was going to be a big surprise for all. She pulled up at the back of the workshop and stealthily crept through the back entrance only to find Thomas with his head under the bonnet of one of the work vehicles. She quietly made her way to where he was and stood behind him, then lay her hand on his butt. He lifted his head. There was only one person that touched him there: he turned around and there stood Briar. He grabbed her in his arms and kept repeating her name over and over, as if in disbelief. "Thank God you're back. I've waited so long for this day, it seems like forever," he said amidst tears. Briar couldn't believe him showing such emotion, as she had never seen this from him before. He must have truly missed her. What would he think if he knew she had given birth to his son?

"Did you miss me?" he asked. She clung to him and pressed her body into his.

"I'll come back to you soon. I had better let the family know I'm back," she said as she broke from his hold. He whispered to her to be quick.

As soon as Briar pulled into the driveway, her mother came running out. "You're home! Why didn't you tell us?"

"I wanted to surprise you."

Their voices brought her father from his office. "When did you get back?" Then all the questions started, and she felt uncomfortable telling untruths once again to her family, but this was an ongoing saga and many more would follow.

Her sisters were at work in their own departments, so she would catch them tomorrow.

"Of course you will stay for tea with us," said her mother. This was the chance for Briar to explain that she had brought back a boarder and her baby, so she would have to go home to them. At this moment she realised she would have to drop the 'nanny' and refer to her by name: Kate.

"Is your boarder paying rent?" asked her father. Briar told him Kate was on a benefit so she was paying a nominal amount, but she would do the housework and cook the meals. This seemed to satisfy him as there were no further questions. Her father was a typical businessman: everyone had to pay their way.

"How do you get on sharing your home with a baby?" he asked. Briar told him she loved the baby; his name was

James, and she would pick him up and cuddle him a lot. Her father was quite surprised by this response.

"You will know what to expect then when you decide to get married and have children. This is probably a good experience for you."

Briar had to excuse herself, and she had to make it to the sanctuary of the loo before her tears arrived. This was her baby they were talking about.

She told her father she would start back tomorrow; she would call in and let Thomas know on her way home.

"I'm happy you used your time off wisely, and saw part of the world," her father told her. This made Briar flinch. It hurt. She had to get away; it was all too much. She couldn't wait to escape back to Thomas. He didn't ask questions; all he wanted to know was if she still loved him.

She and Thomas went into their special room and Briar dropped her jeans and Thomas took down his trousers and kicked off his boots. She didn't want him to touch her breasts as they were still tender, and she did wonder if everything was the same in her private department after giving birth. She was about to find out! Thomas had played this moment in his mind over and over, and now it was here. Lust drew them together and everything seemed to be normal. The excitement was certainly there, as was the enjoyment for them both. He knew he had fallen in love with her and if the circumstances had been different, he would have given up his marriage for her, but because she was the boss's daughter it was never going to happen. He did think that in time she might meet someone of her own age, but this only brought sadness to him, and that was a long way off, if ever!

When Briar got home, the nanny had put everything away and was preparing their tea. She told her what had happened on meeting the family, so they would have to drop the 'nanny' title and refer to her as Kate. They had worked out a suitable wage plus free board, so this was the start of budgeting for Briar. It was not going to be easy, but she was determined to make it work. She had bought a pram so they could take James for walks. He was a placid little soul and was now full time on the bottle as her milk had dried up. It would be the highlight of each day to come home at night and cuddle up with him.

Harvest time again

THIS WAS the beginning of the second harvest season for the girls. Willow wanted to have more input into the winemaking, but she had to be careful not to tread on her father's toes. He had just left on his Irish and United Kingdom pilgrimage to see what the orders were like for the season. Their favourite wine was the Sauvignon Blanc, which seemed to go down well in Ireland, and it was their best-selling wine elsewhere. It was the most popular wine of the moment, although the Pinot Noir was becoming a favourite. There had been so much talk on what her father was going to implement, but it was still a wait-and-see game.

Willow was out in the vineyard early each morning checking on the grapes and liaising with Alana, as she was checking to see there were no pests making their way onto the vines. Rose bushes were planted at the ends of some rows for that very reason. If aphids appeared on the roses this indicated the unwanted pests were around. It was much more convenient for the sprays and manures to be in Alana's shed under lock and key than on the shelves in the workshop. On the walls in her nursery, she had charts indicating what stages the vines were at, when they needed manure and when to apply the sprays. She had her own tractor and spreader to spread the manures, as this was a two-week project as she had many acres to cover. Sometimes she had to call on Briar to help if the weather took a turn for the worse, as there was a spare spreader in their workshop. When the sprays had to be applied, Thomas was the man to call upon. He had all the protective gear, and he could manoeuvre the tractor in the small turnarounds at the end of each row. Alana had not yet been able to manage this.

This season Willow was going to do more trials as her experiment the previous season of hand-picking the grapes versus machine harvesting did not yield the results she was hoping for. She was going to try a new strategy this harvest, still going with the hand-picking but leaving the grapes on the vines a little longer, as the balance of sweetness and acidity was not quite there. She comforted herself with the fact it was trial and error for her first season, but this was going to be her year, as she was determined to produce an award-winning wine. This was foremost on her mind.

Dating was not a happening thing, and although men came and went, she showed no interest. She was always pestering the laboratory team wanting them to come up with new ideas. They found this young generation a lot more impatient than her father's generation. He had done the hard graft buying the land and setting up new vineyards, then selecting the right grapes to suit the wines they wanted to produce. He was keen to pursue the red wine industry, so it was up to him to make the decisions, as the girls were too new to the game. He would teach them over time as it was something one had to study. Overall, he was quietly proud of his daughters working together, but he had instilled in them that the business was a four-way partnership, so respect for each other was foremost. In time it would all belong to the girls, so it was up to them to prove themselves worthy of what would one day become their inheritance.

Only another week and the first harvesting for the season would begin, so tomorrow was the pre-harvest party. Their father had returned from his Irish pilgrimage with good news for this year's sales forecast; it looked to be an excellent year ahead for wine sales. The girls were absent from their workstations today, as they were helping their mother prepare for the party. Alana had invited Timothy to come but he couldn't get the time off work. They called each other weekly, and their friendship was progressing nicely, which made Alana happy as he had stolen her heart. No other lad could match his caring and innocent nature, even when her father suggested she meet other young men by going to local functions, as he wasn't sure whether Timothy was the right one for his daughter. She had given up trying to explain his qualities, as no one was listening, so to her it was a closed book. She knew her own mind. She had spoken with Briar about her feelings for Timothy and she was a good listener. But, then again, no one knew of Briar's secret life, so of course her advice to Alana was to go with her heart: it knew what was right.

Briar had asked if Kate could bring her baby along for an hour or so, so she could meet the family.. She knew Thomas was going to be there so was dying to see how he would react to baby James. She didn't know why he and his wife had no children. Perhaps they didn't want any, and she had never discussed it with him. This would be the first of many harvest parties that James was going to be involved with, as he was the unknown heir to this vineyard.

Briar had schooled Kate up on the home situation so she would know how to react to questions asked by the family. Little did the family know they were going to meet their first grandchild. This tore at Briar's heart – so many untruths up until now with many more to come. When would it ever end? She felt she was living a life of lies, but she found the word 'untruths' easier to deal with, as it didn't seem as harsh as 'lies'.

As they were driving out to the vineyard James was asleep, so the Briar and Kate had time to coordinate their stories again, hoping the situation was not going to become too complicated or uncomfortable. On arrival, the staff were all there with filled glasses sampling the previous year's vintage. The first person to greet them was Briar's mother, so she introduced Kate then baby James.

"What a little darling. Can I introduce him to the family?" she asked.

Kate handed James to her and off she went with the wee bundle in her arms. Briar fought hard to hide her tears. Here was her son being carried in the arms of his grandmother, and she had no idea. Everybody was making a fuss of him as there had been no babies in the family for many years. Briar's father was the next to hold James, and this was when she had to get away. The tears just kept flowing. She went outside into the garden and was soon joined by Kate.

"This is hard for you, Briar, and it won't get any easier as time goes by. You just have to try and be brave." With this she went and fetched a glass of wine for them both. When James was returned to Kate, she fed him his bottle.

Briar spotted Thomas walking in the garden, so she took James from Kate and called to him. When he saw her with the baby he came over. She introduced James to Thomas. "James, that's my second name." She watched as he tickled and burbled baby talk to him, which really surprised her.

"Did you not want children, Thomas?" she asked. His answer shocked her.

"I don't think I can ever father children. We tried for years but nothing happened. My wife thought it was my fault, and neither of us got tested so it was left at that. I would have given anything to have a little fellow like this, but time has passed us by. He is a beautiful little boy, and you seem so good with him," he commented.

Briar had to hold her tongue otherwise all was going to be revealed, but this wasn't the right time or place.

"Yes, I love our little James. He is such a placid wee

soul, and I think I would be a good mum one day." On hearing this Thomas cringed, as he certainly couldn't give her a baby, and he couldn't bear the thought of losing her to someone else.

"Let me carry him back to the house," he asked. Briar watched as he placed kisses on James's forehead. Tears trickled down her face and they didn't go unnoticed.

"Why the tears, my darling? You seem so attached to him," he asked.

"That's the trouble, Thomas; I love this little soul as if he was my own. One day, who knows…." then she stopped. She had already said too much.

"Can you make it to the workshop in ten? I'll be waiting," he said with sadness in his eyes. He wondered if she wanted to be a mother. Of course, he couldn't provide her with a baby, but he could make her happy.

In the following days James was the most talked about subject. Everyone adored him, especially her parents. Her mother asked if Kate and James could come for dinner the next Sunday, for a family gathering as she called it. But it was Thomas who was totally smitten with the little guy.

"You must ask Kate to bring him out again soon. I haven't held a baby in my arms for years; it gives me a real buzz. It reminds me of what I have missed out on." Her heart lit with happiness, for she would certainly ease little James into Thomas's life. It was the least she could do, as he was as much part of Thomas as he was her. Here again the untruths reared their ugly head; she couldn't escape them.

Today she and Thomas were on their first stripping of

the grapes from vines on the gentle slopes facing the early-morning sun. With these ripening first, it provided a rough guide to when the next grapes would need to be harvested. Everything just seemed to fall into line from then on. Willow was right on their case making sure everything was running to clockwork, and that the other harvesters were ready for the next big strip. This was Thomas and Briar's busiest time and they worked long hours, but they still managed to keep each other happy. Thomas was so thrilled that their relationship still continued, and he couldn't wait to get to work each morning, just to be near her, especially as his home life was so unsatisfying. Why they stayed together, he did not know, but it seemed to suit his wife, and he was happy with his set-up, so life just moved on.

Briar did wonder if Thomas and his wife still had sex, but she felt it was none of her business, and what happened outside of the workshop was beyond her control. Perhaps one day it might just come up in conversation, as she didn't want to seem possessive, but she did long to know if she was his only love.

Willow

WILLOW KEPT up with all the knowledge she could muster on the growing of grapes. The one distinct advantage of their vineyard, which she credited her father for, was its location. Because it was once riverbed, the drainage was perfect, and the unique combination of soil, climate and topography had a significant impact on grape flavours. Also, her father knew the grape varieties well, so chose wisely those suited to their region, another big plus. She hoped before too long she would gain a lot of his knowledge to become the head winemaker. She felt her father had too much on his plate, so one day she could relieve him of some of his workload. His most important ability was the marketing; he was a people's person and had the skill to win people over. His friendly disposition drew people to him; his smile was infectious and generated a warmth felt by those around him.

Willow felt she could never be as warmly regarded as

he was, but her goal was not with people, but to produce that award-winning wine. Nothing was going to stand in her way as she felt she had the technical skill and artistic intuition to craft a wine that reflected her vision and the character of the vineyard. This had been her dream for many years, and she was going to realise it. She could remember as a young child standing on the top landing watching as the huge vats were being filled with the season's harvest; it had excited her little heart. She knew from then where she wanted to be, in the winery making the wine. Her sisters had other interests, but wine was her dream.

She couldn't wait to get out of bed each morning, have a quick bite to eat then off among the vines to test the grapes for their sugar levels. Today she had her refractometer to measure the sugar concentration in the juice of the grape. It provides a reading in Brix, a unit representing the sugar content of the grape. Also, she relied on her palate as the final test. When studying for her degree in Adelaide she was taught the palate was a reliable source of taste. She could hear Briar and Thomas flat out on the harvesters stripping the first batch of grapes, and excitement rose in her belly: this was the beginning of her second harvest.

The winemakers and the ecologists in the laboratory wondered if this year, again, they would be pestered by Willow. They hoped she was a bit further on with her ability to understand the work they did in the laboratory, and why their jobs were so important. They were there to conduct tests and analyse to ensure the quality, consistency and desired characteristics of the wine were to the highest standard.

Willow had taken in all she learnt from her first year as a winemaker and working with the technicians. She realised she must have been a pain at times so this year she would look, listen and learn. The first season she had thought she could just walk in and take over, but, no, that did not happen, and it was not about to happen this harvest. It would take several years for her to fully appreciate what had to happen to make a top wine, and along the way many people were involved. Also, there were hundreds of vineyards out there all competing for the same prize.

Today the weather had taken a turn for the worse. The Vanuatuan seasonal workers had finished their job of leaf-plucking the vines so the sun could reach and ripen the fruit. But there would be no ripening today as a cool southerly had blown in, which would put the harvesting on hold. This was all part of running a vineyard, fighting the elements and being put behind schedule. Thomas and Briar had stopped harvesting as all the early grapes were in the winery being processed, so now it was just a matter of waiting until Willow gave them the go-ahead to start harvesting the next paddocks. A cold snap could hang around for several days, so the standby drivers of the other harvesters would now be on hold too. It was annoying for everyone, but the weather cared for no one.

At night Willow spent hours writing down names for her prize-winning wine, She had dreamed up many possibilities, but the winning title had not been decided as yet. She had some top contenders – Fields of Sisters, Woven in Wine, and Vines of Legacy, but her favourite at this stage was Harvest of Hearts. She felt this one told the story of the three sisters and how their hearts were interwoven in the vineyard, all in different areas but each as important as the other. She couldn't claim all the accolades as she loved her sisters and knew it would be a mistake to think it was all her doing, while others were just as involved.

It wasn't only the name of the wine; the label was also an important feature. She would consult her father on this as he was the entrepreneur and had seen hundreds of labels when he judged the New Zealand wine awards. She wondered if a particular colour stood out when all the wines were placed together. From now on she would be more observant and see what caught her eye and why! Next time she was in town she would make sure to visit the liquor outlets to see for herself what she found appealing. In fact, the family were going out for lunch at a popular winery in Blenheim on Saturday so this could be the start. Kate and James had been invited, as everyone loved to have a baby present, then cuddles and kisses could be exchanged. It was as if they were both part of the extended family.

The family had discussed how tolerable Briar was having James living in her home. In fact, Kate had to pull out of lunch at the last minute as she had a terrible headache. Briar was bringing James, so they were to meet at the winery. On the way she stopped the car and opened the back door just to tell James she was his mummy, and she loved him. Not often did she get him to herself to tell him the true facts, but when she did, it was a treasured moment shared between the two of them. These moments brought tears as well as joy. He was a cuddly little boy and loved all the attention he could get. He was sitting up and on the verge of learning to crawl. Briar loved him to bits and she just wished she could share her joy with Thomas, but the consequences were too great at the moment. One day it would all have to come out, but that was a long way off. In the meantime, she would make sure Thomas had access to James, so the connection would be there, and they would not be total strangers when the time arrived.

As Briar pulled up at the front door of the winery everyone was there to meet them, then the stampede happened, but who was the first to lift James out of his car seat? None other than her mother. She unfastened the seat belt and lifted him into her arms, smothering him with kisses.

"How is my special little boy today?" she asked. This brought smiles to his face as he gurgled away. Briar had to turn away, as her mother's words couldn't have been truer. As they all gathered at the table, Briar fetched James's carry cot and sat him in it and fed him his bottle to keep him content while they dined.

"You are such a natural mother, Briar," mentioned Willow. Then her father chimed in. "Briar, you need to get out and mix a bit more, perhaps meet a partner, as you are so good with James. Your life seems very narrow, and you are not getting any younger. You will make a good mother. I see it with the love you give James. Don't build your life around Kate and this little feller. You need a life of your own."

He did wonder deep down if there was something going on between her and Kate, but this thought he kept to himself, as he hadn't seen any indication that this might be so.

"Don't worry, Father, one day I will meet someone, but he hasn't come along as yet."

The harvest season came and went and still Willow had not managed to claim the top prize for her wine. She had placed third in the Chardonay section; this was a start but not the one she wanted. She had decided on the name 'Harvest of Hearts' so that was going to be her signature brand. Her father was proud of her as she was working her way up, although he knew she expected too much too soon. Only he knew how long it took to produce an award-winning wine, as he had done so many times.

Two years on

TOMORROW WAS Alana and Timothy's wedding day. There had been many decisions to work through, as Alana's life was here in the vineyard, meaning Timothy had to finish his job at the college in Auckland and relocate to Blenheim. His father had passed away, so his mother had to go into care. He had to think long and hard about his change in lifestyle, but he loved Alana; she was the only girl he had ever felt close to. They shared a love of nature and the environment. But it was the lifestyle change that worried him most. Could he become part of this opulent society that awaited him? He still had a feeling of insecurity in the presence of Alana's father. He felt he thought Alana could have chosen better.

The wedding would have marquees and all the trimmings. It was to be held at Alana's nursery, a venue she chose contrary to her parents' wishes for it to be held in the beautiful family garden. This was one battle she had won, though many more had been lost. The wedding breakfast would be at the family home after the ceremony, but tables had been set up with bottles of wine so people could mingle with a drink.

Alana felt for Timothy as only she knew how he viewed wealth. A new house had been constructed in the vineyard near her nursery, so this was where they were going to live. Her father had instructed them that they should live on the family vineyard as this was where Alana's future lay. Timothy felt overwhelmed, but then he had never had any material things in his life; he just worked to survive and provide for his parents. Could he cope with his new life? He would need to lean on Alana for a lot of help.

The girls were all gathered at the family home rehearsing their roles for the big day. Alana had hired a wedding planner, so she had given Timothy the low-down on where everything was happening, and where he had to stand when his bride walked down the path.

Kate had James decked out in his tuxedo, a trial run in preparation for his big part in the celebrations. He was the pageboy and had to carry the rings for the bride and groom. Alana had worked frantically growing natives in containers so they could be strategically placed to make a special path, the pathway to Timothy's and her heavenly life together. The new home was going to be their wedding present from the family, but at this stage they had no idea and it would all be revealed tomorrow.

James was the star today as he paraded around in his tuxedo, looking so cute, and now that he could talk, he was like a babbling brook. Briar's eyes followed him everywhere. He had even spent days in the workshop with her and Thomas when Kate had to dash to Australia to help her sick mother. Thomas had made a play pen for James as he wasn't allowed near any machinery. Briar's father insisted on this, as he couldn't bear the thought of this little chap they loved being hurt. Thomas enjoyed him being in the workshop as he would sit him on his knee and tell him stories.

The time had arrived for Briar to know if there was any sexual connection between Thomas and his wife. The atmosphere was right, so she asked him. He looked at her and tears came to his eyes. "No, Briar, my wife blames me for us not being able to have children so that part of my life at home has ceased. She wouldn't agree to have tests so there was no point in my taking them, and we don't know who the blame lies with. That is why you mean so much to me; you make me feel wanted again instead of an outcast. If only we could have met in another time, in another place, even in another world, we could have lived together. Just imagine if your family knew that the two of us had been lovers over these past years, what do you think they would have thought? No, don't even go there, the consequences would be intolerable for both of us. We will just have to continue as we are, but when I cuddle James, I think he could have been our child, but then again, I might not have been able to father a child, so this is a wild dream beyond comprehension."

Briar was shaken to the core. Was now the right time to tell him he could father children and James was living proof of this? She had no right to deny him the privilege of parenthood, but the stars were not aligned and now wasn't the right time.

Briar was so happy Thomas was coming to Alana's wedding as she wanted him to see their little boy all dressed up. In fact, Thomas had to drive Timothy to the airport to meet his mother and brother, as he still didn't have a driver's licence. This would be the first meeting of both families. His brother Ritchie was his best man. He was a totally different person to Timothy, with the gift of the gab and the looks to go with it. He had a degree in law and had done okay for himself, but inside he was not half the man his brother was. He never helped to keep his parents, something that was all left for Timothy.

After the greetings and introductions, they headed back to the vineyard. As they reached the house there was no time to take the guests to meet the family as preparations were underway. They would have to meet at the venue. Timothy showed his brother the suit he was to wear so they both changed into them. His mother had bought a new dress, so she was changing also, as time was running out.

"You lucky bugger, you have certainly nailed it, brother. Does Alana have any sisters?" he asked. When he learnt there were two unattached sisters, he thought the game was on. Perhaps he could steal a piece of this paradise for himself. Was this going to be his lucky day?

Thomas drove them to the nursery, which had been transformed into a picturesque setting with flowering baskets hanging from the nursery walls. A pathway was defined by pots of native plants and at the end was an archway covered in white flowers. This was where he would take his wedding vows. He got his mother seated as other guests were starting to arrive. Timothy had certainly done well for himself, she thought, and she hoped he had found happiness as he had been a good son and now it was his time to enjoy life. As the seats started filling Timothy was beginning to feel nervous as he didn't know how many people were going to be here. He took his mother's hand and squeezed it, just to let her know he was happy she was there for him. Ritchie was wandering around as if he owned the place. Nothing seemed to faze him. Suddenly the music started. This was the signal for Timothy and Ritchie to stand by the archway as the bridal party was about to arrive.

Three wedding cars pulled up and the first people out were Alana's parents dressed to the nines, followed by the bridesmaids and the page boy. Then Alana herself was helped from the car. She looked absolutely beautiful in a lovely white lace gown and flowers in her hair. She took her father's arm, and they walked towards the archway. Timothy was stunned: this was the person he was going to be spending the rest of his life with, and he could not have felt prouder. The bridesmaids were dressed in pink lace frocks and looked beautiful. This did not go unnoticed by Ritchie, and, boy, there were pickings here and he would do alright tonight, he assured himself.

Walking ahead of the bridesmaids was the little page boy dressed in his tuxedo, carrying a cushion with the wedding rings pinned on, just for security, as they weren't sure if he would hold the cushion straight. The wedding party walked down the pathway towards the waiting groom. The celebrant directed them to where they were meant to stand to take their vows. First came the greetings, welcoming everyone to the joining in marriage of Alana and Timothy. Timothy couldn't take his eyes off his bride. Her father walked back to his seat so the proceedings could begin. This was the first marriage of the daughters in the family so it was special, and hopefully two more would follow. Thomas's eyes were fixed on James, who looked so cute in his tuxedo. He just wanted to pick him up and cuddle him, and perhaps that could happen later. Then his gaze shifted to Briar; was this what she should be having instead of a behind-the-scenes love affair with a married man who was years older than her? His heart felt sad, but he couldn't even think of her with someone else, In the end, though, he knew his age would be the deciding factor.

As the wedding planner said her piece, the rings were brought forward so the vows could be said. James was called upon to take the rings to the bride and groom. He walked up to the wedding planner and gave her the cushion and stood and looked at everyone. "I can see you, Thomas. Can you see me?" he called out. This brought laughter from everyone.

The rings were exchanged as were their vows to each other, and now they were husband and wife. It was time for Timothy to kiss his bride. This brought cheers from the guests. Now everyone was free to move around and mix with the bride and groom. Thomas took Alana's parents to meet Timothy's mother, as the bride and groom were being mobbed by the guests. It was a very cordial meeting, as Alana's parents were of a different class to Timothy's mother. She told them they had a lovely place and that she knew her son would look after their daughter as he had done for them, and that he was a good lad with a big heart. Alana's father thanked her for coming and invited her to come to their home for the wedding breakfast. He asked her what wine she would like to taste, and he would bring one over.

"Oh, I don't know my wines. What have you got?" she asked. He told her the wines they had, but she didn't recognise any of the names.

"Just bring me something nice, thank you," she said. He realised then that she wasn't familiar with alcohol so he would get her a glass of sweet wine. He knew they had very little in life and he had plenty, so now was the time to be generous with someone less privileged. He had taken a little while to warm to Timothy, but he could see he was from a background where he had to earn every penny, which complicated his life, but he knew where his true values lay.

Ritchie had introduced himself to everyone, especially Alana's sisters. He was hoping to make an impact on them and had his eye on Willow. She was the stunner of the sisters; he would aim high and if that didn't work then he would try Briar. He edged his way up to Willow and asked her what her job was. When he learned she was the winemaker that was a good start. He asked if she could show him inside the winery the next morning as they were only there for the weekend. Willow was a bit hesitant; she hadn't been come on to like this before. She felt he was a little pushy, but he was very good looking. When she found out he was a lawyer that eased the pressure a little. She was a bit choosier with her men, not that she had been looking. She excused herself and went to see that everyone had a wine. His eyes followed her; was she playing hard to get? Surely there was a spark there?

The wedding party were called to have photos taken and this meant he would have contact with her again. Kate took James up to be in the photos. Alana's mother came over and watched the photographer trying to get James to stand still.

"Be a good boy, James, and have your picture taken, then your mum will have a lovely photo of you to hang on her wall, and so will we," she told him.

Ritchie had his eye on the big fish in this family, but little did he know a little fish had her eye on him. Try as he did to make a connection with Willow, it wasn't going anywhere very fast. She seemed elusive; was it a game or was she just not interested? He would have to be patient until she took him to see the winery. Meanwhile there was Kate, who seemed to have taken an interest in him, and she would do at the moment, so he could flirt with her, hoping Willow would notice. As soon as Ritchie's eyes made contact with Kate, she felt drawn towards him. He was very handsome, flirty and very sure of himself. She hadn't looked at the opposite sex since becoming James's nanny, and once bitten twice shy had been her motto, but was that being forgotten now? She was smitten by his charm. He came and asked her if he could get her a glass of wine.

"That would be lovely. I'll have a Chardonnay."

Away he went and fetched her a drink. As he was making his way back, James followed him. "Mummy, toilet," he said as he grabbed Kate's hand. This was a shock for Ritchie, as he didn't know this was her son and this was an immediate turn-off.

"Please hold my glass until I get back," she called to him. He reluctantly agreed. Kate could tell by his manner that he had lost interest in her, as soon as James called for her. She took him off to the toilet. When she returned without James, Ritchie was still there holding her glass.

"Is that your son?" he asked. What was she going to say? She was lost for words. She didn't want him to lose interest in her.

"No, James is not my son. I am looking after him for a dear friend."

"I thought you must have been married when he called you Mummy. That's good, that is all settled," he replied.

This was the go-ahead signal for Ritchie, so he carried on flirting with her, making her feel special.

It was announced that everyone was to move up to the family home as the wedding buffet was ready. Ritchie excused himself and went to find his mother. When he found her, she was being helped into a car by Willow and her father, as they had offered to drive her.

"Could I get a ride?" he asked. He was told to jump in, so he shared the back seat with his mother. His gaze never left the figure in front of him, as there she sat like a goddess with an air of grace about her. He felt it matched his arrogance, although she would not be easy to get to know, but his self-confidence told him that if anyone could do it, he could!

"What a beautiful home and garden. I bet you all love living here, it is so tranquil," remarked Ritchie's mother as they pulled up at the entrance.

"Yes, this is where our hearts are here in the vineyard. We are a fortunate family to have such wealth. I don't mean monetary wise, I mean having all this available to us. We have our parents to thank as father had a vision and a belief that this was the right place to plant the vines and from then on, hard work prevailed."

"Thank you, Willow, but let's talk about today," her father butted in. "The bride and groom looked radiant as did the bridal party, and little James was so cute. Alana got her wish for the wedding itself to be held at her nursery, and I have to agree it was the right place. I hope this is the start to a happy life for Alana and Timothy."

It was time for Ritchie to make himself heard, hoping to impress Willow.

"Timothy was at the right place at the right time to have met Alana. He has certainly landed on his feet to be part of such a go-ahead family. One only has to look around to see a success story. You are a privileged family."

Silence reigned for a moment before his mother spoke.

"Sadly, our lives were totally different mostly due to a car accident, so it was our sons that kept us. It's not the life we planned but even the best of plans can go wrong, yet we managed to stay together as a family, which is important. I know Timothy will love and care for Alana, and they have my blessings."

"Nicely spoken," said Willow's father.

Willow came around to help Ritchie's mother from the car. While she was doing, Ritchie leaned over and intentionally touched Willow's bottom, passing it off with a 'sorry'. He felt the immediate flinch, but this was not the reaction he wanted. Was it dead in the water before it even started? Was there no future here? He would see what happened tomorrow with the winery visit. He would get his mother set up then look for Kate. She was only second best, but he would settle for her or perhaps move on to Briar if she was not his cup of tea. He wanted a piece of this family, as he was one determined man.

The wedding buffet was set out on tables placed around the garden, with the bridal party table in the middle. The buffet tables were placed near the entrance to the garden so people could help themselves as they came through. Waiters were directing everyone to the food, of which there was plenty, as this family never let anyone go home hungry; they were well known for it. The bridal table was being served by the waiters.

This was certainly the life Ritchie thought he deserved; this was his world, but here was jealousy rearing its ugly head. He thought Timothy was less a man than him, that he was the one that should be here celebrating among all this wealth. Suddenly he spotted Kate so went to capture her. Perhaps his selfish thoughts would disappear, and he would be a bit more forgiving in her company. They went and filled their plates and charged their glasses. The food had to be eaten before the cutting of the cake as it was a hot day, and they didn't want the food to spoil.

Thomas found Jamie among the guests, so he sat him on his knee and said to him, "Who is this handsome dude in his tuxedo?"

"Don't be silly, Thomas, it's me."

"You look so cute; I love you to bits. I wish I had a son like you," he told James with tears in his eyes.

"Don't cry, I can be your son. Kate won't mind," he said, as he wiped Thomas's tears away. This was when Briar came upon them.

"What's going on here?"

"I'm going to be Thomas's son because he hasn't got one. I wiped his tears away, so now he is happy."

Briar's heart was nearly torn from within; truer words could not have been more appropriate at this moment.

Everyone was invited to gather around the bridal table to toast the bride and groom as they cut their wedding cake. Alana looked beautiful and beside her stood her Timothy, the man of her dreams, a simple thinking man but whose heart was in the right place. Only she knew how kind and considerate he was.

"I would like everyone to charge their glass and drink to a happy future for this lovely couple," said Alana's father. "I am so proud of you, Alana, you have chosen the man you love, so we all wish you a happy future, and remember James needs a mate one day."

Cheers rang around the garden.

"Your mother and I want to give you your home as a

wedding present." Before anyone could speak, Alana broke the silence.

"Father, Timothy and I don't expect you to do this for us."

"It is our wish, so please accept it."

Everyone was milling around the bride and groom congratulating them, while Ritchie was in the background stewing. He was muttering to himself, "Fancy anyone being given a home as a wedding present." This made him all the more determined to move in on Willow, but that would be tomorrow's project. Meanwhile Kate would do, so he poured a glass of wine and sought to find her. Along with his charm and the wine it didn't take long to win her affections. She had forgotten the pledge she made to herself that no other man would ever hurt her. But the wine was working wonders, and she was feeling relaxed as she knew Briar was taking care of James tonight. She had seen Thomas and Briar together earlier with James. She was the only person that knew the truth and had been sworn to secrecy about their affair.

As the night progressed, Briar's father was concerned that Kate was not looking after James, that Briar was left with that responsibility. He knew Briar loved James as they all did, but she had a life of her own to live. He went to look for Kate, but she was nowhere to be seen, until in the distance he saw her in the arms of someone. He watched as they disappeared behind the bushes and was concerned as he knew she had been drinking, so he followed in case she needed help. As he got nearer, he could hear laughing and was shocked to see Ritchie and her undressing each other. Would he interrupt? No, it was none of his business; he just hoped she knew what she was doing. What he thought of Ritchie was diminishing; was he taking advantage of someone who was not fully in control? He turned around and went back to the party. He was bitterly disappointed in Kate, a mother who had responsibilities. Who was going to look after James tonight, would it fall back on Briar?

Briar's father was happy when he found Thomas playing with James. He felt sad as he knew Thomas had no children; he didn't know why, buy perhaps they didn't want any, or, worse, they might not have been able to have any. But it was Briar who totally amazed him: anyone would have thought she was James's mother the way she doted on him. He wanted to see his daughter settle with a partner and have a family of her own, as she was a born mother.

"Who is looking after James tonight?" he asked Briar. She told him Kate was.

"I think you had better take Kate home soon as she has consumed too much wine. She is James's mother, and it should not be your responsibility, but in this case it will be. I am a little bit disappointed in Kate's behaviour today."

"For goodness' sake Father, this is a wedding. Surely she can celebrate. Don't be too hard on her."

"But what about you? Your life is slipping away, and you should be out meeting someone. You have so much love to give."

Briar let him know she was in no hurry, that one day

it would happen. With this response her father knew it was time to back off, but he did think there was an underlying issue that was not being addressed. He had wondered if she was in a relationship with Kate, but after what he had witnessed tonight, that thought went out the door.

Everyone partied on until the small hours. Briar had taken Kate and James home at her father's request. Alana drove Timothy's mother back to their home where she and Ritchie were staying until they flew back to Auckland. Ritchie was hanging around after everyone had disappeared hoping to catch Willow's eye, as now the coast was clear since Kate had gone home. He saw her clearing away glassware, so he decided to pour her a glass of wine and ask her to join him for a drink. She accepted as she was pooped; a rest was what she needed for a moment. Ritchie came across with his soft talk about the wedding and how much he enjoyed having met their family, and how lucky they were to have had such a wonderful background, hoping to win some brownie points. Willow was all ears as she loved hearing positive feedback about their vineyard. Unfortunately, at that moment her father saw her in Ritchie's company, and remembering what he had seen earlier, came straight up to her and asked her to help get all the tables cleared as they wanted to go to bed. Willow stood up and apologised to Ritchie and carried on.

"See you tomorrow," he called. This brought a question from her father.

"What have you arranged for tomorrow?"

Willow explained that Ritchie had asked for a tour of the winery, so she had agreed.

"Just be careful. I don't altogether trust him."

She wondered what he meant, but she was a big girl and could handle herself.

Ritchie went home, where his mother was waiting. "What a lovely day. I'm so proud of Timothy, and to think Alana's parents gave them this home for a wedding present. There is such wealth in that family. But he deserves it; he has gone without to help your father and myself and made sure we were comfortable. I am so happy for them both."

Hearing this did little to cheer Ritchie up, and in fact he was quite miffed. Perhaps tomorrow he would make headway with Willow while on their tour of the winery. If this didn't work out, he still had Kate in the background. He had to admit he had great sex with her tonight. She had given her all, which made him feel he was the master and she was his slave. He enjoyed a good partner who performed well, as this gave him the boost he needed. They could have a lot of fun together. The only thing missing would be wealth, but she seemed to be close to the family, so perhaps money could be coming her way! He did wonder where James fitted into the story; if he wasn't hers, then who did he belong to? He decided he would do a little background investigating.

The tour

RITCHIE WAS ready when Willow dropped in to pick him up. The winery was her pride and joy, and she delighted in showing it off. She was masterful as she showed him around the outside of the building, explaining how the gabion baskets were filled with stone from their own property, and they had gathered it themselves from the riverbed. This was followed by the story of the ancestors, and their triumphs in England and Ireland. She was quite the storyteller, and he was intrigued. Then she unlocked the winery door and invited him in. His mind nearly exploded when he saw the rows upon rows of huge vats, and when Willow told him they were full of this year's vintage, he couldn't believe his eyes. He knew they had a huge vineyard, but all this wine, that was incredible; he could see dollars everywhere he looked.

"Come up the landing and I will show you the technical side to the winery."

Ritchie followed her up the stairs. To his amazement, in front of him was a huge laboratory. Willow explained that it was where all the research was carried out on the grapes and their different varieties. It was paramount that all the acidity tests were correct, along with sugar content. It was a complex job to make sure the balance was there to make a first-class wine.

"This is so impressive, Willow. You are such a proud person with high ambitions. I can see it in your eyes that you are an achiever."

This phrase mellowed her, and she thanked him. He knew flattery was the key to win her confidence.

Now it was time to ask questions.

"The little boy who was the ring bearer at the wedding, who does he belong to?"

"James, he is Kate's son. They live with Briar and she has been very good to them. They have become part of our family. We all love him."

"But when I asked Kate if he was her son, she told me he wasn't, that she was looking after him for a friend. I wondered as I heard him call her Mummy."

"No, that's not right, of course she is his mother; she is just kidding you," laughed Willow. There was where that conversation ended.

She took him along further and explained what all the rooms were, offices, lounge and cafeteria. He was most impressed.

"Can we have a coffee together?" he asked. With that she went and cranked up the espresso machine and made them a coffee.

"I know you are a solicitor, Ritchie, but who do you work for?"

He told her he worked for a large law firm in Auckland and he often flew to other cities for work. This did impress her a little. But it was what happened next that stopped it dead in its tracks. He moved close to her and grabbed her, kissing her roughly on the lips, while his hands started roaming her body. This was the last thing she was expecting! She jumped up. No one had ever touched her without her permission; in fact this was the first time she had ever been touched. She had given him no indication that she was interested in him as a boyfriend, so she burst out in rage.

"Who do you think you are, you big oaf? I didn't give you consent to touch me; this is harassment and as a lawyer you will know what I am saying. I would have thought that of all people you would have known better."

With this outburst Ritchie felt embarrassed. His fast come-on tactics were not welcomed by this sophisticated young lady. She was a rich girl, and he should have realised she would not be easy, not like Kate who was a bundle of fun.

"I'm sorry, Willow, I fancied you and I thought you liked me, so to me it seemed like a reciprocal deal," he blurted out.

"Well, now you know what you can do. I'll let you out the door and you can walk home. Nice try, Ritchie, but don't take me as a fool, because that I'm not."

This was the end of anything that might have been between them and he had messed up big time. Never mind, though, as he had a willing Kate waiting in the wings. He could now see that Willow would never have been the fun Kate was as she was too self-centred and a bit frosty.

Today Briar and Kate were driving Ritchie and his mother to the Blenheim airport to catch a flight to Wellington where they were transferring to another flight that would take them to Auckland. Kate and Ritchie were in the back seat together and Briar could see them in the rear-view mirror kissing and touching each other. She worried for Kate as Willow had told her what he had tried on her. She didn't like to burst Kate's bubble as she had expressed her feelings for him, and he was flying out so that would be the end. After sad goodbyes, Briar and Kate returned to the vineyard to pick up James, as he was with Briar's parents while they drove to the airport.

Alana and Timothy were on their honeymoon. Alana didn't want him to feel upset about the cost, so she had booked moderate-priced motels as he had insisted on paying. They were both thrilled with their wedding day as everyone seemed to have enjoyed themselves, especially young James who was a hit with everyone. He was now classed as a member of the family. Briar seemed to be bringing him out to the vineyard more often as Kate seemed to be away a lot. Only her father had his concerns, as he thought she was more of a mother to James than Kate.

Today Briar and Timothy were going back to the marina to see if his theory was still valid, that having wealth didn't make for happiness. He had proved it before and now he was hoping to prove it again. They were taking a nostalgic walk along the pier they had originally visited to see if things had changed in four years. A man was hosing down his launch, so Timothy approached him.

"Nice vessel you have there," he called to the man.

"Are you interested in buying one?"

"Hell no, I couldn't afford something this luxurious," replied Timothy.

"That's the bloody trouble when you have all this money tied up in a luxury item. When you have to sell it because you need the money, no one wants to buy it. It creates a huge headache. Just enjoy life son, and don't get caught up in the hype; it's not worth it."

"Thanks for the advice," said a happy Timothy. Point proven!

His theory on wealth had not changed in four years: wealth was not a base for happiness.

Alana had to tread very careful, as their wedding present from her family had not yet been discussed, but she knew she could expect it to come up any time soon. They visited all the gardens in each town, challenging each other on the botanical names of the plants. Both were real greenies, as habitat and nature were where their passions lay. Timothy was waiting to hear back from Blenheim Gardens to see whether he had the job he had applied for. He thought his interview went well so now it was just a matter of wait and see. The Grammar School had given him a glowing reference on his work ethic, so he was hoping the position was his. He didn't want to hang around the vineyard and be classed as a kept man.

He had this thing about supporting his family, that was his position in life.

He had to iron out with Alana about paying for their home. He wanted to put money away each month and make monthly payments to Alana's parents. He knew she would not be happy with this arrangement, but to him it was his duty to put a roof over his wife's head. He was a proud man. He could see challenges ahead with Alana and her family, but he would stick to his guns. Only one more day and their honeymoon would be over.

Three years on

No one, especially not Briar, could not have foreseen the future of Kate and Ritchie's relationship. It didn't end when he flew out of Blenheim but had grown into a strong affair. She was willing to give him all the love and sex he needed to keep him from straying, with secret weekend flights to Auckland. It could only be a weekend relationship, so that Kate was home for the week to look after James when Briar went to work. It was countdown to school as it was only a month away until James started. Kate had told Briar that Ritchie wanted her to move to Auckland so this was something that would have to be discussed.

Alana was pregnant, much to everyone's delight; the first grandchild was about to arrive. She was happy she was able to work right up until she was about to give birth and then go back to work once the baby was born, as she could take it in the pram to the nursery. Timothy had got the job at Blenheim Gardens and was now head gardener and was loving his job. At the weekends they would both go out and plant natives wherever possible, to make the property look loved and cared for. They were an asset to the vineyard, and this was recognised by Alana's family.

At last Willow's dream had materialised. Her signature wine, Harvest of Hearts, had been nominated as the best up-and-coming vintage in the Sauvignon Blanc range. She knew she would get there one day, but it had taken much longer than she anticipated. Her father knew her dream was not going to happen straight away, but he didn't want to dampen her enthusiasm. She, like all the other eager beaver newbies to the wine world, had to learn 'Rome wasn't built in a day', that good wines took time to nurture and mature. Sometimes it was luck and the weather that played a big part in getting the right results.

Willow still hadn't shown any interest in the opposite sex, but now that her dream had materialised, perhaps she could find time to socialise a bit more and meet someone. Her parents were so happy having James around, but soon he would be going to school, and they couldn't count on Kate being around forever. James would then just become a memory to them; this was upsetting just thinking about it. They needed a youngster around, as it was something to focus on other than the vineyard. James had brought them the most joy they had experienced lately, but now with Alana's baby on the way, this was welcoming news. This would be their first grandchild and with this position came a family inheritance that was passed from one generation to the next, to the first born.

A tragic loss

Discussions between Briar and Kate were making for a strained friendship, as Kate wanted to move to Auckland to be with Ritchie. This caused a headache for Briar. Her love for Thomas, and his for her, was stronger than ever, even more so since James came on the scene. Thomas secretly thought of him as his and Briar's, the son he never had. Briar wondered what was going to happen when Alana's baby was born, as it would be the first known grandchild of the next generation. The inheritance was not an issue; James would not be acknowledged as a member of his rightful family, if the truth didn't come out, but she had to protect Thomas.

They still had their sex sessions in the workshop. Sometimes it was a hurried affair, but Briar loved it when they had time to explore and have fun. She was the mistress on the side, and he was the married man in a high position, so it had to be kept a secret. She loved the role play; she could be whoever and Thomas loved her playful antics. He loved her completely. She could never look at another man, much to her father's disappointment, as he saw her as a nurturing, caring mother to be, as she had strong maternal instincts. This came to the fore with James.

Tonight, there were harsh words between Kate and Briar, as she wanted to be released from her nanny role to begin a new life with Ritchie in Auckland.

"I will give you a fortnight to sort something out, Briar, then I am leaving. I'm sorry. I'll miss you and James, but I have a life of my own to live."

Briar was shocked. What would she do? She had lived a life of untruths, so were they going to catch up on her?

As she was driving to work the next morning stress overcame her, and the tears started until they became uncontrollable. She couldn't see the road ahead through her tears, the road became a blur, then suddenly there was a loud bang … then nothing. There had been an accident, a car had crossed the white line into the path of an oncoming milk tanker. The tanker driver tried to swerve but it was too late, as his vehicle had jack-knifed and blocked the road. He was shaken, but what had happened to the oncoming car? It was nowhere to be seen. How many people were in the car? He knew it was a bad accident, and that there would be fatalities. Traffic started to pile up and people were coming from everywhere, but shock had set in, and the driver just froze in his seat. It wasn't long before a police car arrived and next thing, he knew was he was being questioned. The police had called the fire brigade as they needed cutting gear to rescue anyone inside. The car was a mangled mess, and only one person could be seen inside the car, in the driver's seat. There didn't appear to be anyone else in the vehicle, but that would only be established when the fire brigade arrived. Meanwhile the police were getting information from the tanker driver as to what happened. He said he tried to prevent the accident, but the oncoming car drove straight into his path, and there was nothing he could do. The motorists who were gathering were asked to go back to their cars, as by now it was established the driver was deceased. When the cutting equipment arrived, there was relief that the driver was the sole occupant of the car.

A woman from the line of cars approached the police and told them she recognised the car and knew who the deceased would be. They were thankful, as now they had some identification of the victim. The information came from a neighbour who passed Briar each morning as she was coming to work. The ambulance arrived and took the tanker driver away to hospital, as he was still in shock and required treatment. After finding out who the next of kin was from the neighbour, and where they lived, a second police car was deployed to speak to the family.

As they reached the approach to the vineyard, they followed the road until they arrived at the workshop. They stopped and went in through the back door, calling to anyone who may be there. Thomas, of course, was the first contact.

"We are looking for a Mr Morrisey."

When he saw the uniform, Thomas panicked. Briar

had not arrived at work. She was late, which was most unusual. Why were the police here?

"Has something happened to Briar?" he asked.

"We have to talk with Mr Morrisey before we can release any details."

"But Briar works here with me. She is a mechanic; she hasn't arrived at work yet." The officers stood for a moment, but decided the father had to be the first to be notified. Just as they were about to leave, in walked Briar's father as he had seen the police car and thought something had happened at the workshop.

"How can I help?" he asked.

"Are you Mr Morrisey?" When he confirmed who he was the police asked him to sit down.

"There has been an accident along the highway, and we believe it involved your daughter. She crossed the white line into the path of a milk tanker. Unfortunately, she didn't survive. She is being cut from the wreckage at this moment. A neighbour recognised her vehicle and gave us this address."

"Where is Briar, Thomas, is she at work?" asked her father.

It was at this moment when Thomas knew he had lost the love of his life, the tears flowed and shock set in. When he didn't answer, realisation hit Briar's father, and he cradled his head in his hands.

"My darling daughter, my darling daughter," he kept repeating amongst his sobs. Thomas went over to comfort him and put his arms around his shoulders.

"How did it happen?" Thomas asked the police.

"Apparently the car crossed the white line, and the tanker driver tried to swerve but it was too late. The driver has been taken to hospital as he is in shock."

The police expressed their condolences and if there were no further questions, they would return to the scene of the accident. Through his grief Thomas thanked the police, then offered to drive Briar's father back to the home to inform the rest of the family.

After all the family were told, they were grief stricken. Alana was so shocked she went into premature labour and had to be rushed to hospital. Timothy was still at work, so they had to call him to meet them at the hospital as he didn't yet know about Briar. Apart from the grieving family, Thomas was suffering. He had lost his lover who meant everything to him, and now he was left with nothing but memories. Was he going to be able to continue at the workshop if his Briar was not going to be there with him? It took a moment for him to remember all the wonderful times they had together there. He remembered the first time they had made love; it was Briar who instigated it. He had initially refused but that didn't deter her. She had asked him to be her first-ever lover, to teach her, as she was still a virgin. The memories just kept pouring in. He had to stay here in the workshop, as this was where it had all happened, and he could stand and dream in the places where their passions had run wild. Suddenly he thought of James. Would Kate move away and take him with her? Surely, he wasn't going to lose him too.

Thomas asked the family if they had let Kate know, but

in their grief they had forgotten to inform her, so he asked if he could let her know, to which they agreed. He drove in silence, still processing the loss of the love of his life. When he reached Briar's home he walked to the front door and knocked.

"Can I come in, Kate."

Once through the door he asked her to sit down as he had some sad news.

"There has been an accident. Briar's car crossed the white line in the path of an oncoming milk tanker,"

"Oh my God, is she okay?"

"No, Kate, she has passed away, she died instantly."

"This is all my fault," she cried out. "We had an argument last night; I gave her an ultimatum of what to do with James…" then she stopped. Thomas asked her to explain what she meant.

"I know the row we had last night upset her. I feel sick. What are we going to tell James?"

Thomas told her not to worry, that he would pick him up from his playgroup. Perhaps it was not the right time to tell him. A moment passed before Kate realised the consequences of Briar's death. James was not her son, and no one would know this, so what decisions would she make? Although she loved him, she had told Ritchie he was not her son and for that reason their friendship flourished. 'Oh my God, what a mess,' she told herself. Who would she give up, James or Ritchie? She couldn't have them both. Kate sat with her head in her hands, crying and consumed with guilt over Briar's death.

Three days passed, and Briar's family had been to

identify her body, They could not believe she was not here anymore. She was the loving one of the family, the one who loved James so much, and he was going to really miss her. Her father was absolutely devastated. He had hoped she would meet someone one day and become a mother; she would have been the best. Funeral arrangements were underway and as one life was taken another arrived. Alana had given birth to a girl, so sadness was mixed with a little joy.

Briar's solicitor contacted the family to say he had Briar's will and asked that they come to his office the following afternoon. The family never even thought of her leaving a will as she was so young. He also contacted Thomas and asked him to come at 10.30 in the morning as he had an envelope for him from Briar. First thing next morning Thomas was at the solicitor's office to pick up the envelope. When he was handed the envelope, the solicitor told him he knew of its contents, and if at any time he wanted to discuss anything with him, he would be available. Thomas thanked him and left. He sat in his car and pondered what the contents would tell him. He couldn't wait any longer so tore it open. In the envelope was a birth certificate. When he saw his name as James's father, 'What the hell' he said to himself. Accompanying it was a letter explaining everything, why she couldn't tell him for fear of him losing his job and being cast out by her family. This is why she had made James part of his life, so he would never be estranged from him. 'You were the love of my life, Thomas. James was our love child, now he is yours, forever Briar.' He was overcome with grief, but nothing seemed to make sense: when did she have James? How did this all happen? Was he really James's father? He thought he couldn't have children, and his wife blamed him for them not having a family.

As Thomas sat in the car things started to ring true. He thought back to before James was born and Briar had gone on an overseas trip for four months. Was this when she was pregnant? Was she alone when having the baby, and why wasn't he there to support her? Why didn't she tell anyone, not even her family? Do they still not know? He was beside himself, and he had to know if she had told her family, so he went back to the solicitor's office. The solicitor told him Briar didn't want her family to know who James's father was and it was not recorded in her will.

"They will find out that James was her son, but it stops there. It is up to you as to what happens from here on, so good luck. All I can say is she protected you to the end."

He would wait until after Briar's funeral as no one knew they had been lovers. When they found out, he would probably be sacked but at least he had a beautiful son as a reminder of Briar; he still had part of her.

Today, a day before the funeral, Briar's family had an appointment with the solicitor. They were welcomed and offered a seat; Alana couldn't come but Willow was present. The solicitor started by telling them that Briar had left her inheritance to her son James. The family were in shock. No, that wasn't right; he was Kate's son.

"I think you have got that wrong. James belongs to Briar's flatmate Kate," offered Willow. The solicitor then proceeded to tell them that Briar was sorry for all the untruths told, but James was definitely her son. Absolute shock took over, and no one spoke. Who was the father? Briar wasn't even dating anyone, so, no, this was a mistake.

"Are you sure of these facts?" asked the father. "When did she have the baby? She was overseas when he would have been born."

"It is all explained in a letter. Briar told me what happened, but I was bound under the Privacy Act not to disclose anything until she was no longer with us. She wanted me to tell you she was sorry for all the untruths she has told through her life, but she didn't mean to upset anyone. She loved James's father, who was the only man in her life, and she didn't want you to know because of the upset it may have caused."

"Then who is James's father?" asked Willow.

"I'm sorry, I can't disclose that information. He has just been given James's birth certificate, and like you has just found out. It is up to him to talk with you when he is ready."

Briar's father asked, "But James will come and live with us on the vineyard. We will be his guardians, surely."

The solicitor told the family that decision would be James's fathers to make, as he was his legal guardian. There was silence. None of the family was prepared for any of this, but James could not be taken away; he was the only piece of Briar they had left.

"Please take the letter home and read it as a family, as everything is explained, then perhaps things will be easier for you to digest. I'm sorry this is a sad time for you all. Briar wanted your forgiveness, never for one moment thinking her life was going to end so soon."

The family thanked the solicitor and made their way to their car, still in shock. So many questions. Where did they begin? Nothing at this stage made any sense. But one thing was strong in their hearts: if James was Briar's son, then he belonged with them, he was their grandson. But where did the father fit in, and who was he? Briar hadn't been dating anyone!

On their arrival home Willow called Alana to come immediately as they were holding a family meeting to read Briar's last letter. After the letter was read, tears streamed down everyone's cheeks, and sobs were heard as they learned what had happened to Briar, her lone journey through childbirth, with no family members to support her. It left them stunned. She wasn't overseas enjoying herself; instead she was going through her pregnancy on her own, but how and why? Did Kate know the whole story? No wonder Briar appeared to be the nurturing mother; she was the mother! Now they could see why James had been brought into their lives. He was part of them, their flesh and blood, and Briar wanted him to be accepted as such.

The family would talk with Kate and see what she wanted to do. Only close family and the permanent workers were invited to attend the funeral as the family were so distraught at losing Briar, they couldn't face lots of people. They just wanted to get it over so they could bring her ashes home where she belonged. Kate was coming around tonight so they could discuss what was going to happen to James and herself. He was still with her until after the funeral.

During all the funeral arrangements no one had even thought of discussing James's father, but this subject was best forgotten as the parents wanted control of him. He belonged to their daughter and therefore, in their eyes, he belonged to them.

Kate arrived with James to Briar's parents' home as arranged. Willow and Alana were also there. James ran to everyone and hugged them; as yet he hadn't been told of Briar's passing, as Kate couldn't bring herself to break the news to him. She hoped maybe the family could do it now that they knew the truth. Alana let him have a little nurse of baby Jessica, hopefully to soften the blow. James asked where Briar was so now was the time. Briar's mother lifted James on to her knee and told him Briar was not coming home as she had gone to live with the angels.

"But I want her here with me. They can't have her," he cried.

"We all want her here to live with us, but the angels needed her, so she has gone to them," said his grandmother.

"Won't I ever see her again?" he sobbed. They all told him there would be photos of her everywhere so they would never forget her. How was he going to cope with the thought of losing Kate as well? This would have to wait until the grieving for Briar was over. Kate told the family she was leaving and going to live with Ritchie in

Auckland. "Why didn't you tell us the truth about Briar?" asked Willow.

"Briar hired me to care for James. She was my employer. I couldn't go behind her back as she helped me when I came back from oversees. I had nowhere to go."

"Were you with her when she gave birth?" asked the family.

"No, just after. She had no one; she went through it all on her own, and she was very brave. She didn't want to bring shame on her family, because she loved James's father dearly."

Now the burning question: who was James's father?

"I'm sorry, that is not for me to disclose. I promised Briar. She was my saviour, and I will never break my promise to her. All I know was he didn't know about James, and I don't know if he does to this day."

Now the family had to discuss what was going to happen to James tomorrow. He was too young to attend a funeral, so Kate agreed to stay at home with him. Then it was arranged for him to go to his grandparents for a holiday. This would allow Kate to take off to Auckland without goodbyes to James as she was afraid he would be traumatised to know he was going to lose her also. A new life awaited him.

It was tears all round for Briar, but it hit her father the most as the family carried her coffin into the church. She was the first one of this generation to have passed, something that was not expected for many years, so it was a sad loss. With her went so many secrets: the birth of her child, the father's name, and why it had to be hidden from the family. That's what family was for, to be there when needed, so why did she feel she couldn't come to them when they loved her dearly? But the truth had to be hidden to protect Thomas.

This was a dreadful day for Thomas and he was an absolute wreck. He had lost his lover, the only person in his life that made him happy, who loved him for who he was. But now he knew out of his love for Briar had come James, their love child. This had taken him by complete surprise, but he had a piece of Briar that would always be his. And like the family, he was sad that she had gone through the birth all on her own with no help or support from her loved ones.

His life would never be the same, but it did prove one thing, that he had lived many years being blamed by his wife for them not having any children. Since Briar's passing, he couldn't continue living with his wife, so he asked for a divorce, before it would be known publicly that James was his son. No one apart from himself was going to share their lives with James. He didn't know how her family would handle hearing he was the father; he wasn't sure what to do himself! But today was about Briar. It was a sad day. He looked for James, but he wasn't to be seen. He asked Alana where he was, and she told him the family decided it would be too much for him, so he was at home with Kate.

Thomas burst into tears.

"But he should be here; this is his mother," he blurted out.

Alana was taken aback by Thomas's outburst. How did

he know about Briar being James's mother? Only the family knew at this stage. Why was he so upset she wondered, but of course, they had worked together in the workshop for many years, and she would have been like a daughter to him! The church was silent as the service began. The minister gave a brief eulogy but none of the family could speak because they felt too devastated. Her sisters felt broken as part of them was lost forever, and they were triplets no more. But part of her remained and that was in James; he was her soul. Now they understood why she spent so much time with him and how much she loved him, which was something to treasure.

After the service finished, the people attending were invited to the family home for tea and sandwiches. It wasn't a celebration of Briars life; it was goodbye to a beautiful daughter who had left too soon. Briar's father made an announcement that she had left behind her son James and her soul would live on through him. On hearing this, Thomas had to leave. He wanted to hold his son to feel the love that made this child as he held him close. He drove fast to Briar's home where Kate was minding James. As soon as he saw Thomas, he ran to him and held on to his leg.

"Hi, Thomas, did you know Briar has gone to live with the angels? They needed her, but so did I."

This was too much for Thomas. He picked James up and held him close to his heart, sobbing like a child.

"I love Briar as much as you James and I will miss her too. One day I will tell you a little secret that will make you happy."

"Tell me now, Thomas," he pleaded.

"No, not today, because we are all sad. I love you, James. You are very dear to me; we will see each other every day when you holiday with your grandparents. You can call into the workshop when you come home from school."

James clung to Thomas. "I love you too, Thomas," he said.

Kate asked James to go outside and play as she wanted to talk to Thomas. She told him she knew about him and Briar but had not told the family, because she didn't want them to know, solely to protect him. It was all too much for Thomas, to think Briar loved him so much she had protected him and suffered herself. This was a love that could never be broken, and when the time was right, he would claim James as his son. Kate told him she was going to Auckland to continue her relationship with Ritchie and that James was going to live with his grandparents.

Thomas said, "Because James is losing the two most important people in his life, I will just let this plan go ahead at the moment, as James is starting school in two weeks' time. He doesn't need any more shocks; he is still so young to cope with what is happening. I will ask one thing, though. I want to buy his first schoolbag. I will go and buy it now and I want you to tell Briar's parents that she had bought it before she passed away. That way, as his father, it will be my first present to my son. The grandparents will probably want to do that, but I want it to be my privilege."

Kate agreed to Thomas's wishes. This would be the

beginning of the father–son relationship, albeit behind closed doors at the moment.

When Kate took James out to his grandparents to begin his holiday, she took his schoolbag with him, as requested by Thomas.

"But we have bought him one," said his grandmother.

Kate told her Briar had bought it before her accident, that she wanted him to have it on his first day. Kate hoped they would accept this, as it would make Thomas happy. As James's next of kin, it should be his place to buy his son's first schoolbag, but of course only Kate and Thomas knew this, and it would stay this way until James was settled into a routine.

Thomas would see James every day once he was at school, as he had asked him to call into the workshop on his way home. This way he had contact with him and could ask him if he had any problems that needed to be attended to. It was breaking his heart that this had to be held from James as he wanted him to know he was his father. He missed Briar and cried every night; he couldn't come to terms with knowing he would never see her again. It was only James, their love child, that gave him the strength to continue living.

In the workshop when he went to their special love spots, his eyes filled with tears. The memories of Briar's wild passionate lovemaking, her eagerness to please him, to make him feel warmth that he had never experienced before their love affair began, tore at his heart. It was to be no more … she was the love of his life and from this love came James, who one day would come and live with him so they could be a family.

Alana and Timothy

ALANA AND TIMOTHY and baby Jessica were settled into their new home. Timothy had saved and bought a little car to get him to work each day. Alana had taught him to drive, as until he got his licence, she had to drive him to work. It was just a little runabout as he was putting money away each month to pay Alana's parents' back for their home. Her parents argued with him, telling him it was a gift, a wedding present to them both, but this fell on deaf ears. He had an issue with being 'a kept man', he had integrity, and he knew the home would never feel it was his, if he didn't pay for it. Alana tried to explain to him it was given to them as a wedding present, but he couldn't get his head around this way of thinking. He was brought up to believe people had to earn what they owned; nothing was just given to them. This was going to be an ongoing debate between this young couple.

Alana took Jessica to work with her each day, as all she

had to do was push the pram a couple of metres down the road. She loved Timothy as he was caring and always offering to help with their daughter, but she still sensed an air of doubt by her family that she could have found someone from a similar background. One thing was for sure: he wasn't there for the money, and the family acknowledged this. He wasn't a fortune hunter, but it was his independence that frustrated them most. He was not a social person and didn't attend wine events held at venues, or even ones at their winery. The family did not understand his thinking, even just for Alana's sake; surely he could have made an attempt to please her? This was cause for concern, but their daughter seemed to be happy so in the end that was all that mattered.

Today was daughter Jessica's first birthday. All the family were invited to their home for the party. Uncle Ritchie was staying with them as his romance with Kate had ended. Although she had supplied him with all the sex he needed, that's all it was, as his thoughts were elsewhere. He realised sex without feelings amounted to very little, and it was Willow who held his heart strings, not for her wealth but for something deeper. He knew he had made an absolute fool of himself the day they visited the winery, when he tried to come on to her. At the start all he saw was wealth, but he soon realised it was more than money, it was feelings that he had never experienced before. With Willow's aloofness and her determination to succeed, he could see a bit of himself in her. They both liked the party scene and were outgoing people. Unlike his brother who he thought bordered on boring, the wine world excited him. Because Ritchie had left home and went to Auckland to work, their lives were total opposites.

Jessica had just started walking around things and her best friend was James. He made her laugh as he did funny things. He would visit her every weekend and play with her. He pushed her in her walker and encouraged her to walk so she would grow up and play bigger games with him.

Alana's parents along with Willow and James arrived with a supply of wine to celebrate, as Alana had done all the catering. Willow had no idea that Ritchie was staying with Timothy. Up the driveway came one of the winery tractors pulling a trailer that was covered by a large tarpaulin. Timothy went out to investigate, and upon looking under the tarpaulin he was shocked, as there was a beautiful playhouse. It was Jessica's birthday present from her grandparents. All he could see was extravagance. Why would they give her a playhouse for her first birthday? She could barely walk without help. He was not at all happy, as he felt he was being deprived of making one for his daughter when she was old enough to play in it. He didn't want to cause an upset, but he would talk about it later with Alana, as the party was just beginning. James was excited about Jessica's party, and he asked if Thomas was coming. No one had thought to ask him, which was a slip-up, so Timothy phoned him. James had settled in at school, and although he had suffered when he knew Kate was gone, as the days and months went by, it became easier for him, and he also became Thomas's friend. He would call into the workshop each day on his way home from school.

As yet James's father had not appeared on the scene, so it was assumed by Briar's family he didn't know or he wasn't interested in his son. This played nicely into the hands of his grandparents as now he was recognised as the first grandchild. With this came the inheritance that was given to the first born of each generation. Timothy was happy about this as he didn't want his daughter given money for nothing, as it wasn't earned. And for James to be the first male born since his grandfather was another plus. Everyone loved him as he was their reminder of a daughter and sister taken too soon; her soul lived on in him.

As Willow made her way to find Jessica to give her her present, she was shocked to run into Ritchie. Her heart missed a beat as she remembered his brazen attack on her. At the time she had been annoyed, in fact angry, but as time passed, she never forgot his forthrightness, his bold decision to act without her consent, to be the leader and take things into his own hands – so self-righteous!

"I hope I have earned your forgiveness," were the words that greeted her.

"I hope you have brushed up on the laws around harassment."

As much as she wanted to tell him he was out of order back then, she smiled and walked on to find Jessica. "Perhaps she has forgiven me," Ritchie thought to himself. She didn't snap at him, so he presumed all was well between them. He decided to play the hard-to-get act and be conspicuous by his absence. He went to the back lawn where James was kicking a ball around on his own, so he asked if he could join him. Laughter rang out between them as they tried to steal the ball from each other, which drew Willow's attention. She stood in the shadow of a veranda post watching the little kid playing with the big kid. While watching, she saw a different side to Ritchie, one that quietly pleased her. Was she drawn to him because he was a bad boy? Was it excitement she was after? Until now she had never met anyone that excited her enough to begin a relationship with. As she was classed as a growing force on the wine scene, perhaps this kept possible suitors away. Ritchie was very handsome and a party boy, so was this the man she had been waiting for? She knew her father wasn't keen on him, but for what reason she didn't know.

Everyone gathered and watched Jessica unwrap her presents. James stepped forward and helped her rip the paper off, so he could see what was in them. He seemed more excited than Jessica, but she was still a baby so didn't seem to understand. Willow had bought her her own personal gift of a desk and little chair for her to use when she grew older. Most of her presents were future orientated as she didn't need much at the tender age of one. Then they were all asked to come out to the driveway to where the tractor sat. Alana's father took off the tarpaulin and underneath was a professionally made playhouse. It was painted pink and white with its own little veranda. Gasps came from those gathered. It was enough to upset Timothy, as he thought it was over the top. James, on the other hand, was delighted, whereas Jessica was too young to appreciate it. 'For goodness' sake, who at one year old needed a playhouse' was Timothy's uppermost thought. This extravagance had to stop; he didn't want his daughter growing up expecting a life of luxury. He knew Alana was used to all that was given to her by her parents, and he couldn't take that away from her, but his daughter was going to be brought up in a realistic world, where she had to work and earn to buy things. Little side issues were starting to creep into their marriage and Timothy was determined to stand his ground.

James found Ritchie and asked if they could continue playing with the ball, as he was waiting on Thomas to arrive. When he appeared, Ritchie had other matters to attend to, so he excused himself. Thomas loved this father and son time, and it was precious to him, as it was getting closer to him wanting him to bring him home and be a family. He needed to feel warmth in his life, and James was his nearest and dearest. The tears still flowed every day for Briar; they never ceased. He had photos of her everywhere in his home waiting for James to come home then they could both talk freely about their love for her. He was going to ask his boss if James could come and spend a weekend with him, just so he could get a feel of how the future might pan out.

Meanwhile Ritchie was hot on the trail of Willow, and although he promised himself to let her make the first move, he had to be in a place where this could happen. He walked around the house until her caught a glimpse of her nursing Jessica. She looked at home with the little one sitting on her lap; was he warming to the thought of children? Until now kids were not on his agenda, but the more he had to do with James and Jessica a feeling of warmth and understanding were beginning to appear. He stood and watched her, and his heart started beating a little faster as he thought of how things might be one day. His breakup with Kate left her with a broken heart, but as he explained to her, sex without feelings was not a good basis to build a long-term relationship on. It was Willow who was constantly on his mind; she was the one he was mentally making love to while having sex with Kate. Would he or would he not begin a conversation? No, he would be breaking his own rules, but weren't they made to be broken? This was a common occurrence in his life. As one rule was broken another one was soon introduced. He was a man of action and if a broken promise were to happen, then life just went on.

As he was about to make a move, Willow stood up and turned around, and on seeing him she came over.

"What are you doing down here? Where is Kate?" Ritchie was caught off guard. He wanted to give an intelligent answer, but he was lost for words ... a rare moment indeed!

"Can I get you a glass of wine? Then we can sit down and have a chat," he answered. She nodded in agreement. As he went to get the wine a lot of past moments kept popping up in his mind, ones he would rather forget. He couldn't afford to stuff up this meeting.

As he walked back with two glasses, she suggested they

go out onto the patio to talk. James and Thomas were still playing with the ball and laughing.

"Did you enjoy playing ball with James?" Willow asked Ritchie.

"I didn't realise you were watching. Yes, he is a great wee kid, so full of energy and happiness, when it could have been so different for him. He has accepted his losses with such bravery. I guess he keeps Briar's memory alive, which is wonderful for the family." Willow was most surprised by his statement; he had certainly grown up since their last meeting.

"Kate told me the whole story. It brought tears to my eyes but at least she had the chance to be a parent despite being so short; she did have some precious time with her son."

"Did Kate mention who James's father was?" asked Willow. Ritchie told her he didn't know as Kate had made a promise to Briar, and she would not break it. From here on conversation flowed freely between them, until they were called to sing happy birthday to Jessica. They all gathered around the dining room table and sang while Alana cut the birthday cake.

Thomas was asked to bring the forklift from the workshop so they could lift the playhouse off the trailer. James left with him and, hand in hand, they went on their way. Within five minutes they came back with the forklift, with James sitting on Thomas's knee as proud as punch. Timothy was busy working out where to put it. He was still annoyed, and he would speak to Alana once all the guests were gone and let her know he thought it was ridiculous the amount of money spent for a first birthday. He knew it would cause an upset, but he wanted to be the provider for his family. He did think it would have registered with Alana by now, but he was beginning to think he couldn't change old habits. It was the wider family that was the problem, and money was readily available. But what Timothy overlooked was they had done the hard work and now the family were reaping the benefits. Perhaps the marriage was a mismatch; only time would tell.

Willow's change of mind

TIME WAS PROGRESSING FAVOURABLY for Willow and Ritchie; he was very selective with his words as he couldn't afford another falling out. Willow jokingly asked him if he had brushed up on the harassment laws, to which they both laughed.

"I am deeply sorry. I humiliated myself, but I hoped you had forgotten that by now." Then he thought to himself, "If she remembered, then she must have been thinking of me."

"What are you doing later?" asked Willow. Ritchie had nothing on, so he let her know. "I have been invited to a prize giving this evening; would you be interested in coming with me?"

"If that's an invite, then I accept."

Willow said she would pick him up at 5.30, which only gave them an hour to get ready, so she left in a hurry.

Ritchie had time to rush and have a shower and get

dressed and it wasn't long before he heard the toot of a horn. Parked in the driveway was Willow in her black Mercedes. She was a bright, intelligent person, and he was looking forward to accompanying her to whatever it was they were going to.

As he climbed into the car, she greeted him with "I have brought you along tonight to drum up votes for my wine. Tonight, six finalists are going to be judged, and the winner receives flights and accommodation in Melbourne."

"If I drum up the winning votes then I expect you to take me to Melbourne with you," he told her.

Willow nodded in agreement, at which he nearly did a back flip. This was a huge incentive for him, so, yes, he would go all out and do battle for her.

They made a fine couple as they arrived at the cellar door venue. Ritchie was as handsome as she was beautiful, and the combination looked a winner all the way. As they walked past the six selected wines on display, there was Willow's Harvest of Hearts standing proudly alongside the others. Each contestant and their partner had two bottles of wine of which they had to take around and offer to the crowds to taste, and then they had to select their wine of choice. This was a People's Choice competition. This meant a lot to Willow, as her next ambition was to win such an award to stand alongside her award for 'best up-and-coming wine of 2004 award.

She had certainly picked a good marketer to promote her wine. Ritchie walked around the crowd full of self-confidence, and this reflected in his ability to win people's hearts. Willow looked on in surprise. He certainly knew how to promote the product, people listened to him, he had a persuasive manner, and his looks were part and parcel of his sales pitch. She did notice several of the younger and not so younger ladies were drawn to him, and this annoyed her a little. Usually this would not have worried her, but tonight it was different, and she admitted to herself there was a bit of jealously creeping in. But why, she asked herself; she had never felt like this before, she had never met anyone that had this effect on her, so why now? It was hard for Willow to allow her heart to warm to someone, as she had only thought of herself up until now.

She made her way to Ritchie and drew him away from his admirers by asking him to get her a glass of wine. With a glass in her hand, she introduced him to some winemakers.

"I didn't know you had a partner," said one of her competitors.

Willow looked at Ritchie and winked. "We have known each other for nearly two years now. See, people don't know what goes on behind closed doors. I play it close to my chest."

"You are a bit of a mystery; no wonder none of the local lads stand a chance," he said as he studied Ritchie. This remark pleased her; Ritchie seemed to be getting the approval from her circle of acquaintances.

"Time for the 'People's Choice'," announced the judge. This was done by a show of hands which were counted by the referee who then recorded his findings. Willow's Harvest of Hearts was the last to be voted on. Up went many hands. All participants waited in anticipation as the referee counted the recorded hand shows. The judge called the finalists to come up on stage and stand behind their bottle of wine, then the winner was announced.

"The winning count goes to the winemaker of Harvest of Hearts. Congratulations, please come forward and accept your prize."

A proud Willow stepped up to collect her award and her prize amid a cheer from the crowd. No one was prouder than Ritchie. He had done his job, so did the offer to accompany her to Melbourne still stand, he wondered. Did she keep promises or was she like him and let them slip by and replace them with the next one?

Willow came to get Ritchie and introduce him to the judge. "You did well, son. Your sales skills certainly won you popularity among the crowd. What is your profession?" he asked. Ritchie told him he was a lawyer.

"You take your young lady to Melbourne and have a wonderful time; you both deserve it," he said.

Ritchie looked at Willow to see her thoughts on this statement. She just smiled without making a comment.

"I hope you are not going to renege on your promise."

"You will learn that when I say something, I don't go back on my word, so, yes, we are off to Melbourne."

Thomas

The harvest season was not far off, and Thomas needed help. Briar's position had not been filled. It was hard for the family to think about a replacement for their daughter as it was for him, but he wasn't able to carry on without a replacement. He insisted they employ another mechanic to help with the machinery before the next harvest began. While talking to his boss, he asked if it was possible for him to have James stay for a weekend. It so happened the whole family had been invited to a wedding in two weeks' time, so he was delighted that Thomas could have James while they went away.

The days couldn't pass fast enough for Thomas, as his heart ached to have his and Briar's son living with him, even if it was only for a weekend to start with. Perhaps the tears would stop, and he would feel warmth back in his heart. Life had been very empty for the past several years and his love for Briar had never diminished, not one little bit. If it hadn't been for James, he had contemplated ending his own life; he was the thread that held him together.

The day had arrived. It was Friday and James would come home from school as usual and call in at the workshop, then at 5.30 they would go off together to Thomas's home. They were both excited, but not for the same reasons. This was an adventure for James, but for Thomas it was a homecoming for his son. As they pulled up the driveway and stopped the car, he leaned over and took James's hand. "Welcome home, James, I hope you will enjoy your time with me this weekend."

"I love you, Thomas. You are my favourite friend."

This nearly broke his heart, to be his favourite friend was beautiful to hear, but above all, he wanted to be called 'father'.

As they went inside, the first thing that took James's eye were all the photos of Briar. He stood and looked at them; they were everywhere. He couldn't help but wonder why. "Briar's photos are everywhere; I love these photos. You must have loved her like I did, Thomas."

He could hold back no longer, the tears flowed uncontrollably. Here was his family, James, Briar and himself, together at last.

"Don't cry, Thomas, Briar will see you," said the innocent little voice. Thomas knelt down and hugged James, telling him that apart from him, Briar was his second-favourite person.

Over the weekend they did any things together and Thomas's heart was filled with joy. He had never felt so happy for years, and life had a meaning again. He had thought happiness had eluded him forever. To think all his married years he was blamed for being sterile, when in fact he could have fathered children. Why wasn't he brave enough to own up to his affair with Briar? Perhaps if he'd done so, she would still be alive today. So what if they were outcasts, they loved each other, and nothing else would have mattered. Now he had their child, who was his reason for living. Briar would love him for this!

Tonight was their last night together, so Thomas wanted to ask James some questions, but without being too nosey.

"I hope you have enjoyed your time with me. Would you like to come back again?" James was quick off the mark. "You must feel sad living here on your own. Perhaps Grandad and Grandma will let me stay with you, and we could both play ball together. They are too old to play ball with me, and you could be my father, seeing I don't have one."

"But you do have a father, who no one knows about except you, me and Briar. Briar was your mother and I am your true father. This is the little secret I wanted to tell you."

"Why didn't you tell me sooner?"

"Your grandparents don't know so we have to keep this a secret for a little longer. That's why I have all the photos of Briar; we loved each other. It is a long story, and I will explain it all to you one day. I love you, James, that's why I wanted you to call into the workshop each day so I could see you. Briar didn't want to tell your grandparents about us, as I was only a worker on the vineyard, and I was a lot older than her. But I can't hide it any longer. I want you to come and live with me, so the three of us can be together again; we can be a family."

"No wonder I loved you, Thomas. You are my father. That's cool, and now I am like all my friends and have a real father. Can I sit on your knee and cuddle you?" he asked. "You can cuddle me anytime, James. You are my son and I love you dearly."

They sat together and cried.

"Can I call you Father now, not Thomas?"

Thomas explained they would have to wait a little longer until he told James's grandparents. It was not going to be easy as he would probably lose his job at the workshop.

"But they can't do that to you, Father."

"Please be patient, James. You can call me Father each day in the workshop after school, and when the time is right, I will talk to your grandparents. Would you be happy to come and live with me?"

"I want to have a father. I love you Thomas. You are my father, and I should be living with you and looking after you."

After Thomas tucked James into bed, he lay beside him and told him all about Briar and himself and how much he loved her. All the photos were on the walls so he could see her each day.

"When I come and live with you, you won't be lonely anymore and you will be my father," said a happy James.

"Remember you told me a long time ago you had a secret to tell me, now I know."

Thomas kissed him goodnight. Tomorrow, he would drop him off at school on his way to work. As he walked down the hallway, he lingered at every photo and told Briar that James now knew he had a father and soon they would be a family again.

Several applicants had applied for the mechanics job on the vineyard. The boss had interviewed them and the one he chose was a young man in his late twenties. He had two thoughts in mind: finding a worker and a future son-in-law. He was hoping there would be a spark between him and Willow. He could see she was getting to be set in her ways and if this continued, she would never find a man.

At the moment he only had two grandchildren, James and Jessica, but Alana and Timothy were expecting their second child. They wanted many more grandchildren. He had no idea of Willow's newfound fondness for Ritchie. He would not be pleased, as this he would class as a not-in-a-lifetime chance, before it even got off the ground. He would certainly not see him as a potential candidate for his daughter. Not after what he had seen on the evening of Alana and Timothy's wedding day.

The grandparents' noticed James was spending more time than usual at the workshop with Thomas. He wasn't just stopping for half an hour but sometimes they would have to call him to come home. Today he was told to come straight home, not to stop off at the workshop.

"But I like Thomas, and he needs me as he is lonely. He only has the photos of Briar to look at," protested James.

"What photos do you mean?"

It was then James realised this was his and Thomas's secret, so he wouldn't say any more. After James had left for school, the grandparents pondered his comments about the photos of Briar in Thomas's home. Why would he have them? They concluded that because they had worked together for several years, he must have missed her like the daughter he never had, so no more was mentioned ... case closed.

The new mechanic was a nice young man, so hopes were high that Willow might be attracted to him. A new harvest season was approaching so all the machinery was ready to go. Thomas seemed pleased with the new guy's work ethics. He couldn't wait until James called into the workshop as now James always called him Father. This was their secret as James loved the concept of having a father, just like all the other kids at school. Sadly, because of the new mechanic he would have to tell James to stop calling him Father when he was around, and he was sad as he knew how disappointed James would be. But this did not happen as James never called into the workshop. Thomas worried he might be sick as this was most unusual; he had never missed a day.

The next morning when his boss came into the workshop, Thomas asked him if James was not well, because he hadn't seen him today.

"No, he is fine, but we thought he was spending too much time here, so we told him to come straight home."

Thomas was upset: was this the start of an uncomfortable relationship with his boss? Despite all the years they had worked together, was it all starting to fall apart?

"But I enjoy hearing how James's days are going at school. He tells me everything, I really missed him yesterday," said a desperate Thomas.

"We have decided that he will only be calling in every second day from now on, that will be Tuesdays and Thursdays."

This meant Thomas would only see his son for two days a week. He wondered how James felt about this arrangement; he would ask him tomorrow.

That night he went home a dejected man. He talked all night to Briar's photos, asking her if it was time to come out in the open with their affair. He was James's legal guardian and had more rights than the grandparents. No way were they going to stop him from spending time with his son. Perhaps it was time for the truth to be revealed, but at what cost – his job and his long friendship with Briar's family?

The next day couldn't pass fast enough for Thomas: only half an hour to go before James walked through the door. He so wanted to hear what James had to say about them only seeing each other two days a week. Half an hour seemed to take ages, then suddenly, he heard James's voice.

"Father, I'm here," and he ran to him for his cuddle. This did not go unnoticed by the new mechanic. Thomas didn't have the heart to tell him not to use 'Father' in front of him, the time was not right, and he knew James would feel disappointed. He didn't want him to feel any more hurt.

"I've missed you, son. I wish we could see each other every day." This left it wide open for James to have his say.

"I'm sad, Father. Why can I see you only two days a week? Don't you want to see me?"

"I love you, James, but your grandparents think you spend too much time here in the workshop."

"But I want to, and you are my father, Thomas," he cried. Thomas lifted him up and they held on tight to each other.

Yes, the time had come for everyone to know the truth. They needed each other now that James was growing older. He told James he would come and speak with the grandparents on Saturday, and they would tell their little secret. Then James could come and live with him.

Lives change

IN THE MEANTIME, the new mechanic was baffled by the emotion-filled meeting between Thomas and James. Why did he live with his grandparents when he had a father? Willow had been asked to stop off at the workshop to pick up the mechanic to take him to the winery as her father need him to do a job. Again, this was a two-way thing, trying to coax Willow to like his pick of a young man for her. While she was driving him, he asked why James wasn't living with his father.

"We don't know who his father is. Our sister passed away before she could tell us, so it's a mystery to us all. We would love to know."

"Then why does he call Thomas, Father? They were hugging each other in the workshop today; it was really sad."

This information shocked Willow, and she didn't know how to answer.

"Are you sure?" she enquired. The mechanic told her the conversation that had taken place in the workshop. Things went very quiet. He knew then he had spoken out of turn; what would Thomas think of him for spilling the beans? He had no idea of the situation, and it was really none of his business as he didn't know all the circumstances, but now it was too late.

That night after James had gone to bed, Willow asked her parents to sit down as she had some news for them. She heard something from the mechanic, she couldn't make sense of it, but perhaps they might know.

"What did you hear?" asked her father. Willow repeated what she had been told.

"But why would James call Thomas Father. It must be in fun, and perhaps he thinks it will make things easier for him," suggested the grandmother. This did not go down well with the grandfather.

"I will not allow this to happen any longer. I will speak with Thomas tomorrow. James is our grandson, Briar's son, and he is the only connection to her we have left. It must end here," he ranted.

The next morning the boss came into work and asked to speak with Thomas in private, so the mechanic disappeared as he had a fair idea what was going to happen.

"Thomas, it has come to our attention that James is calling you Father. We are not happy about this, and we ask you to discourage him from doing so in the future. I will talk with him and explain this is not to happen."

Thomas was totally devastated; James was his son, and he didn't want him to have to go through any more hurt.

"Boss, can I come to your home and have a meeting with your family. When would be convenient? Please don't say anything to James in the meantime," he pleaded.

"James is our grandson, so I am going to talk with him," was the reply.

Silence followed then everything got the better of Thomas. Now was the time; he couldn't hide it any longer.

"I'm sorry you have to hear this, but James is Briar and my son. This is going to be hard for you to understand, but we loved each other. I didn't know until she passed away, when the solicitor gave me James's birth certificate, that I was named as his father. Briar must have wanted me to get to know my son and that is why she brought him here so often. I love him dearly and…"

"But, Thomas, you were a married man; my daughter was just a child and you ruined her life. I would have given you more credit than that, and to do this to me and my family is disgraceful. She wouldn't have known it was wrong, but you did. I can't believe you have done this to our family."

"I'm sorry it has come to this, but we loved each other. I begged her to find someone else her own age, but she said she would never love anyone else. She told me she was on the pill, that's why I knew nothing about James."

"I am in shock: my daughter with our mechanic who is years older than her, you were old enough to know this wasn't right. We will not give up James; he will live with us." Thomas was not going to let this pass him by.

"I'm sorry, boss, but as James's father I am his legal guardian, and I want him to come and live with me."

"That will never happen, Thomas. James is the only reminder we have left of Briar. How do you think the rest of the family are going to take this? They will be devastated like me. She was just a child, and you took advantage of her. Take your tools and get the hell out of here. I never want to see you again."

Thomas stood his ground.

"This is the exact reason Briar didn't want you to know, as she was afraid I would lose my job. I tried to end our affair several times because of my respect for you, but she begged for me to stay with her. The saddest part about this whole thing is that she had James on her own without any of us there to support her. That breaks my heart as she was torn between her family and me. She didn't want to lose either of us."

There were no more words to be said, so Thomas picked up his tools and walked out. That night a family meeting was called by Briar's father. No one knew anything about what had just happened, so this was going to be a shock to everyone.

"Today I learned who James's father is and you are not going to believe what comes next. Thomas told me he and Briar had been having an affair for a couple of years and James is their child."

There was shocked silence.

"But that can't be. He was a married man and much older than her; what would she see in him? He should have known better," sobbed Briar's mother. Alana could not believe that they were lovers; she had just thought they were good friends. It wasn't that she disliked Thomas, but it all seemed a very sad story. She could have had anyone as she was a lovely person with a vibrant personality.

"Oh my God, what will happen to James, will Thomas want him to live with him? Why didn't he say anything sooner? What did you say to him, Father?" asked Willow.

"I told him to pick up his tools, that I never wanted to see him ever again."

"But, Father, we need him; he is the only one who knows how everything works with the harvesting. Where are we going to find someone else at this stage? He has been with us for years, and our new mechanic knows nothing about the vineyard. If Thomas was Briar's choice of a man and he made her happy then that's all that matters. At least she experienced happiness in her short life and she gave us James with Thomas's help."

"Why are you so forgiving? I can't believe Thomas did this to our family. We have treated him well," said her mother.

"Yes, Mother, and he has been very good to us. Who else is going to be on the harvesters at 4am to bring the grapes in before the heat arrives? He is needed here, so you and Father are just going to have to be accepting of him. What you don't realise is he could just walk off with James, and we might never see him again, then Briar's soul will be lost to us. Please think sensibly about this, as we have more to lose than Thomas. Imagine how much he is suffering losing Briar. Now we know why James mentioned the photos of Briar in his home."

The room went silent: it was time to think of the overall picture, to let the shock settle then look to the future. Willow's father paced up and down the hallway. Perhaps his daughter was right; there was the thought that they could lose James because if Thomas had no job, goodness knows where they might end up. He couldn't imagine life without Briar's precious son as he was the one who carried her soul and kept the family memories alive. Besides, harvesting was only days away and they had to get the grapes off at the right time.

"I will go to bed and think on this; I have always treasured Thomas's input into this winery, and his heart is here. I just have to process what has happened and work out what is best for us all," sighed the father.

"Yes, let us all sleep on it, and see how we handle tomorrow," replied Alana.

The next day began with dark clouds. Heads were still all over the place and the breakfast table was unusually quiet, as James noticed.

"Why is everyone sad today; have I done something wrong?" he asked.

His grandfather was the first to answer. "I'm sorry, James, for stopping you from going to the workshop yesterday after school. You can go there whenever you want to talk with Thomas."

He jumped up from the table and ran to his grandfather and hugged him.

"Thank you, Grandfather. Thomas is special to me, and we have a 'secret'," he said with excitement. The family looked at each other, for here was their answer. If they wanted James to be part of their lives, then Thomas had to come back to the workshop. "Thomas is taking a couple of days off, so he won't be at the workshop," replied James's grandfather.

"Is he sick? Does he need me to look after him?" James asked.

Again, this cemented to the family the fact that Thomas's job had to be offered back to him. Now that the family knew the 'secret', that Thomas was James's father.

"I will take you to school this morning, James, as I have to go into town." With this he jumped into his grandfather's car. Everyone was there to say goodbye as they knew where he was going; the decision had been made.

As he pulled up outside Thomas's home, he took a few minutes to compose himself as he had been very blunt and unkind to him. He walked up to the door and hesitated before he knocked. It seemed to take ages for the door to open, and when it did, there stood a devastated man. His eyes were bloodshot, and his face tear stained. The two men stood and stared at each other.

"Can I come in please, Thomas? I need to talk with you."

As he walked up the hallway, everywhere he looked there were photos of Briar. As he entered the lounge there were more photos. He had never seen so many. He stood and stared at them, and the tears started. To have so many reminders! It was then he realised that Thomas did really love her, and he missed her as much as they did. Before he could say anything, Thomas spoke.

"I cry every night for her. Apart from James, all I have left are her photos. The reason I didn't tell you sooner is I wanted James to be properly settled after losing the two people who mattered most to him. He was so young to have suffered the way he has. He knows I am his father; I told him the weekend he came to stay with me. He wanted to know why all the photos of Briar were in my home, so then I gently told him our story, that Briar was his mother, and I was his father. He was so happy; he couldn't wait to tell the kids at school that he had a real 'father' just like them. He was so proud, that's why he called me Father in the workshop. I'm sorry you had to find out this way, and I know the family will hate me, but Briar was the love of my life."

Upon hearing these words, Briar's father was torn. How could he have been so unkind to someone whose whole life had fallen apart, just like theirs?

"I'm so sorry, Thomas; it was just the shock that made me so angry. I know in my own heart that Briar was happy. She was such a maternal person and now we know why. She deserved to live a full life, but sadly that didn't happen. My family don't hate you, and we would all like you to come back to work. You are part of our family and no longer the missing link. It was in anger that I told you to go. Take a couple of days off then come back. We need you, Thomas." With these words the two men hugged each other and parted. On his way home the grandfather realised they hadn't discussed James's future, but first things first; that could wait.

The Melbourne trip

THE WEATHER HAD DECIDED to have a cool break, so the grapes were also on hold, as they needed the hot winds to come again along with the sun to do the final ripening. This was time for Willow to sneak off to Melbourne for her People's Choice prize, but only for four days then she had to get back. No one knew Ritchie was part of the deal, and no one needed to know was Willow's thinking. Today she was flying from Blenheim to Wellington then to Auckland to meet up with him. She was secretly happy about the whole adventure as she hadn't seen him since the award night, and he had had to fly back to Auckland the next morning.

She liked the way he talked with everyone and managed to sell her wine at the tastings. He was flamboyant, as well as opinionated, and people liked what they saw, including himself. She surprised herself recognising these qualities in him, as at first, she thought he was arrogant and a womaniser. But with his good looks he was always going to attract the opposite sex. She had no idea where this friendship was going. Neither had found the partner of their dreams and time wasn't standing still; they were both getting close to their thirties, so was this to be the start? Were they too fussy? Willow certainly was.

On their arrival at the hotel, they were welcomed and given the key to their apartment, which was on the twenty-fourth floor. As they entered, it was all very nice and then they saw the two queen beds. Willow chose her one and put her suitcase on it, so that left Ritchie with no choice. They both kicked off their shoes and flopped on the beds so they could make plans for the evening. It was decided they dine in the hotel restaurant, as they were tired and a good night's sleep was what was needed, ready to hit the town tomorrow. Willow unpacked her suitcase and hung up her clothes. On seeing this, Ritchie remarked on the amount of clothes she had brought for only a short stay.

"One day, Ritchie, you will understand that women need a choice of wearables when on holiday."

"I've never been on holiday with a lady before, so it looks like I am about to learn."

"Well, I'm taking a shower before dressing, so the bathroom is mine for the next half an hour."

"Why do you need to shower for that long?" he asked.

"You're learning Ritchie, never ask a woman about shower time," and with this the closed behind her.

He lay on the bed thinking: she seemed to be talking in

riddles. She was most unusual, and he still had no idea where he stood with her. So far so good, there had been no disagreements, but then again, he was on his best behaviour. He wouldn't come on to her and make a fool of himself; that had happened once, but never again. He did wonder, though, what would happen when it came to bedtime. He had dreamed of this moment sharing a room with her; was that all that was going to be shared?

When she finally came out of the shower, she looked beautiful, with make-up on and hair was all flossed up. All she had to do was settle for something out of the wardrobe. He was hoping she would let the towel slip to expose what was underneath, but instead she picked an item and headed back into the bathroom. "Your half-hour is up. Now it is my turn," he called to her in jest.

"You're welcome to come in anytime, Ritchie, I'm not stopping you."

Was this an invite or was she bluffing? He decided not to take her up on this remark; it was too early in the night.

They made their way down to dine, and Ritchie felt privileged to have her by his side as she looked amazing. He had told her so before they left the room, and she playfully kissed him on the cheek. Ritchie suggested they go to the lounge bar and have a pre-dinner drink. A waiter asked for their drink order, then asked them if they were on their honeymoon. Willow answered, "Not yet, but perhaps one day. He hasn't asked me to marry him. I'm still waiting."

This took Ritchie right out of his comfort zone; what was she implying? Willow noticed he was uncomfortable.

"Have a laugh, Ritchie, let yourself go. Let's have a bit of fun."

Right at that moment he thought to himself, if she was here for fun, then fun it would be, but later.

After they had eaten, they went to the bar for a drink. Willow asked if she could have a glass of Harvest of Hearts wine.

"I'm sorry, but we don't stock that wine; in fact I have never heard of it. Where is it made?" the barperson asked. This was Willow's cue to promote her wine.

"It is a lovely Sauvignon Blanc from the Marlborough region of New Zealand. In fact, I am the winemaker, and it was voted the top up-and-coming new wine for 2024."

"Oh, we will have to look into stocking that," he said. Ritchie felt there was more promoting to do.

"Two weeks ago, it was voted the People's Choice wine at a cellar-door venue, and that is why we are here, as we won the award and this was the prize."

The barperson offered his congratulations.

"That was great, Ritchie. Your sales pitch will take you far," remarked Willow. After a couple more wines Willow was on top form, resting her hand on Ritchie's leg. He wasn't sure if she knew she was doing this, if she was in fact coming on to him, but the call was hers!

"Who wants the bathroom first," asked Willow as they made their way into their suite. She was feeling a bit tipsy so decided she should go first.

"But just a minute, that's hardly fair, you had it first last time," said Ritchie in jest.

"Well, we can share, I just need the bathroom for a

minute, then you can come in." Ritchie waited then he heard her calling, so he went in. There she was half undressed; her dress was on the floor, and she was standing in her undies and bra. "Oh, I'm sorry, I'll go out," he said.

"You don't have to go. Have you never seen a girl in her underwear before?"

"But this is inviting trouble if I stay," answered Ritchie.

"Then trouble it will be. Come here, you daft man," and with this it was full on. He carried her out and lay her on her bed. He could not believe this was happening. She had let her guard down, and underneath all the pretence was a desperate woman. She begged him to undress her, to take off her bra and knickers, then make love to her. He wasn't going to let it be over before it got started, so he gently caressed her. He let his hands work her body while she writhed around begging to be taken, but he wanted to savour the moment. He had wanted to have her from the moment he set eyes on her, but at first it was for all the wrong reasons, and now he knew why. This was why he had to let Kate go, as their sex was just that, with no meaning for him, a loveless relationship that didn't satisfy him.

His body was building up to the moment when she would be his; excitement was running through his veins, and this would be a moment he would never forget. As he entered her, she let out a cry of delight and hung on to him as if she was afraid he would leave her.

"I'm going nowhere my darling, tonight has been my dream since I first met you."

"I have to tell you, Ritchie, until tonight I was a virgin." He could not believe she had never had sex before.

"I'm sorry, I didn't know. I would have been gentler with you."

This was how the first night was spent, in Willow's bed. When she woke in the morning she reached over and cuddled into Ritchie. She wasn't sure who made the first move, she couldn't remember, but it was probably him. She waited until he stirred then challenged him.

"I hope you know I am taking proceedings against you for molesting me," she said.

"I'm sorry, Willow, but you were the instigator last night. If you hadn't begged me to undress you, then this would not have happened."

It was time to put it all back on her, to make her feel the guilty one.

"Never mind, it was fun, and you are a good lover, Ritchie, but then I knew you would be. You have that special charm that makes a girl feel wanted. Actually, we are a good pair, bits of snob, aloof and secretive. Obviously, she had given this a bit of thought before last night's hi-jinks. Did she need that little bit of alcohol for encouragement to bring her down to thinking like an ordinary person, or was it because it was her first time?

Today it was up and about, first breakfast then on to some sightseeing. They hired a private driver to take them to special places as their time was short in Melbourne. They wanted to cram in as much as possible. There had to be a day's shopping for Willow, so Ritchie decided to go to the casino for the afternoon. He was not a great gambler but every now and again he would have a punt, and, besides, shopping bored him, especially clothes shopping, and knowing Willow it would be a painful experience. He loved her choice of clothes; they were feminine, and she wore them well. She had the height and the figure to look good in anything. She was the prettiest of the three sisters and the last to settle, which was causing her father some concern.

This was their last night together, as they flew out the next day. Ritchie had not made it to his bed, as he decided her bed was more exciting than his, and she seemed to agree. The last three nights were full on, and they learnt a lot about each other. Willow came across as a prim and proper miss, but under the bedclothes she was a different person. He wondered if she felt she could be herself unseen but had a façade to portray to the outside world. This was probably due to her ambition to be the best winemaker. She had secrets to keep from potential rivals, thus making her a little unapproachable if one was not close to her, or didn't know her.

He decided to take her to a wine-tasting gala tonight as a surprise. It was a white-collar event, so he asked her to wear something special. He had brought his tuxedo. Willow commandeered the bathroom for the next thirty minutes, so this meant Ritchie could be dressed by the time she emerged.

When she saw him, she was mesmerised. He was the perfect picture, the complete picture in her eyes. He was such a handsome specimen, she didn't want to share him with anybody, and in fact she wanted to undress him right there and then.

"Please, Ritchie, let's stay and have fun, just the two of us."

"No, Willow, I'm taking you somewhere special – you'll love it. You look fabulous, you will be the star," he announced.

To her there was only one star, and he was hers. She would make sure no one came anywhere near him! As they waited in the foyer for a taxi, all eyes were upon them as they looked like an A-list couple. A lady came up to them and directed conversation towards Ritchie.

"Who are you and what movies have you been in?" she asked.

He laughed and told her he was just an ordinary bloke. She then turned to Willow and told her to keep an eye on him, or he may be stolen from beneath her feet. This further cemented her feelings; he was definitely the one for her. She was beginning to realise she had put herself on a pedestal, when in fact she was just an ordinary person, but this had been a long process for her to come to terms with. Because she had become too involved in the quest to produce that award-winning wine, her sense of reality was not normal. But the wait was worth it, and she had found the missing link at last.

The red carpet was crowded with people attending the venue. The dress code was adhered to and everyone looked glamorous. It wasn't until they arrived in the foyer that Willow knew what they were actually attending. Again, her passion was to the fore; she loved the hype and buzz within the wine industry. It was announced the wine awards would be given out as soon as everyone was seated. These were top Australian awards so she would get a fair idea what type of wine was the most popular one, here across the Tasman. Ritchie had secretly contacted the event organisers and told them why they were here, so this was going to be a surprise for Willow. They were shown to a table where two other couples were seated. They looked a little older than themselves, and did they look the part, with jewellery sparkling. After introductions, it took a little while for them to warm to Richard and Willow, perhaps because they were Kiwis. There were several bottles of wine on the table, so Ritchie asked which one they recommended. Neither couple were connected to the wine industry, but they supported the industry and that was evident in the number of times they replenished their half-full glasses. Willow's eyes never left Ritchie; she was lost to him completely, spellbound to say the least, and she wished they were at home having fun in her bed. But now that she was here, she had to enjoy herself, as this was a gift from Ritchie.

It wasn't long before Willow noticed one of the women was sly glancing at Ritchie all the time, something to which he was oblivious. She left the table to go to the bathroom and when she returned, she had reapplied her make-up. As she sat down, she moved her chair to be closer to him. Willow knew then she had a rival, an older but a lovely-looking lady, and very well spoken. She would keep her eye on this one! The awards were being handed out to the recipients who came up onto the stage to collect them. Each winner thanked everyone for supporting them by buying their wines. Then an announcement was made.

"We have a special guest here tonight all the way from New Zealand. She is here because she won a People's Choice award, the prize for which was a holiday in our lovely city. She has also crafted the best up-and-coming wine of 2024. Please welcome Willow Morrisey to the stage."

"Ritchie, how did they know I was here. No, you didn't, you told them!" whispered a shocked Willow. Ritchie lifted out her chair so she could make her way up, amid the claps and cheering from the audience.

"Welcome to Melbourne, Willow. We hope you have enjoyed our beautiful city. Can you please tell us the name of your award-winning wine?"

She couldn't believe this was happening; it was all too much. It took a few seconds for her to find her voice.

"Thank you for the warm welcome; your city is indeed beautiful. We have crammed so much in our short visit, and we will be back. I am here with Ritchie my partner who has been a great support person. My wine is called Harvest of Hearts, a Sauvignon Blanc. If you ever come to New Zealand please try my wine. Thank you!"

As she was about to sit down, she noticed a hand on Ritchie's lap. He didn't seem to make any attempt to remove it, so she would keep her eye on this. It didn't take long for the hand to move closer to his crotch, and this was when she reached across and removed it.

"Come, Ritchie, I want to go home," said Willow.

"No, you can't go," said the people at their table. "They are only halfway through the prize-giving." Willow cast a disapproving look at the offender then decided it would be rude to walk out. She asked Ritchie to move closer to her, away from the other annoying cow. Now it was her turn to put her hand on Ritchie's knee, hoping the other one would see he was out of bounds to her, or any other female. Then she had a thought, why didn't he move the stray hand away from the prowling advances of the other woman? Was this always going to be a problem when they mixed with other female company? She knew he was a drawcard; who wouldn't want him?

As they were leaving, the offending female slipped a card into Ritchie's jacket pocket which didn't go unnoticed by Willow. She leaned over and whispered very quietly, "He's mine, so keep your grubby hands off," to which she just smiled at Willow, much to her annoyance. Willow took hold of Ritchie's arm as they headed out to flag down a taxi to take them back to their hotel. She wanted to say something to Ritchie about the stray hand on his knee, but she would wait until they were on their own as she didn't want to cause a scene. It was decided a nightcap would be fitting seeing it was their last night, so they stopped off at the hotel bar. Willow decided on a cocktail while Ritchie ordered a whisky.

"When did you let them know at tonight's venue about me?" she asked. "I will have to keep you on as my fulltime PR person; you did me proud."

"I just wanted to spoil you. I've had a great time; you mean a lot to me, Willow. I know we started off on the wrong foot, but we have both moved on. Otherwise look what you would have missed out on!" he said in jest.

"If it wasn't me, it would have been someone else. You don't seem to be short on admirers," she replied.

Ritchie could see a smidgen of jealousy creeping in. He told her that since Alana's wedding he had Kate, but because he had deep feelings for her, he had to let Kate go, as it wasn't fair to string her along. He hoped this would give her some reassurance. On this note she took his hand and led him to the lift. When he took his jacket off, she reached into his pocket and took out the card, placed there by the other woman. Upon reading it she was totally gobsmacked; it was a personalised card carrying the name of a well-known media personality. Written on it were the words, 'Meet me later tonight in the foyer. I know where you are staying.' Now was the moment to ask Ritchie why he didn't remove her wandering hand. Ritchie looked her straight in the eye, "I knew you were watching so I wanted to see what you would do. Don't worry, it would not have gone any further, I promise you that."

Was it enough to convince her? He hoped so.

"Willow, you don't give anything away with words. It is hard for me to judge how you feel as you can run hot and cold, something I'm not used to."

With this said, it must have hit the spot as she came up to him and admitted she was jealous and didn't know how to handle it.

"This is all new to me, Ritchie, I have never felt this way about anyone before so I'm finding it challenging, and my emotions are all over the place. I have only had myself to think about, but since meeting you that has all changed."

Tears welled up in her eyes, she was losing control of herself and felt vulnerable.

"It's okay to express how you feel, and now I know, it makes it so much easier for me. Trust your feelings and everything will fall into place."

Ritchie was seeing a different person when she felt vulnerable and let down her guard; she was actually an ordinary girl who had a lot to learn about life. They sat on the bed, and he comforted her by holding her in his arms. She needed to be rescued from her emotions as they were alien to her.

Ritchie went to the bathroom and when he came out, she was in bed. He asked if she wanted to sleep on her own tonight, for some space. She reached out and asked him to make love to her. She needed to feel loved, to feel she belonged to him. She watched him undress; he was very pleasing on the eye, and it was no wonder she fell for him. He pulled back the bedclothes only to find Willow already naked. He cuddled into her, making her feel relaxed, then he pressed his body into hers. She could feel the outline of his manly part; it was ready to perform but it had to wait, as he wanted to caress her to build up a passion that would bring them together as one.

Now that Ritchie knew how she felt about him, making love was more meaningful, he could think of her as his, so a more playful approach could be taken. It was not a 'having to please scenario' but was 'let's have fun'. They laughed and teased each other until the moment of togetherness overtook them. Willow whispered a 'thank you' in his ear as now she felt comfortable enough just to let go and be there in the moment.

The last goodbyes were sad for them as Willow had to leave Ritchie in Auckland. They didn't know when they next would meet as Ritchie had a high-profile embezzlement case to file to the court, so he had to be in his law office every day until it came before the court. And Willow would be right into the harvesting season, so it was a busy time for them both.

"I will call you tonight to see you arrived home safely," Ritchie assured her.

As she was driving home from the airport to the vineyard Willow had never felt so happy. It was a different happiness to what she had ever known. Her other known happiness was the wine industry, but this was completely different. Then came the sudden jolt back to reality; how was she going to explain Ritchie to her family, especially her father, as she knew he didn't have much of an opinion of him. She didn't know why as there had been no reason for this dislike that she knew of.

Everyone was there to greet her as she pulled up in the driveway. James was the first to reach her and gave her a big hug and told her he missed her.

"Guess what, Willow, I'm going to stay with my father for the school holidays, isn't that just wonderful? We will both be able talk to Briar in her photos."

"I've missed you too little James, and I'm happy for you," said Willow. It was only then she realised how much she had really missed him; he was Briar's legacy, and everyone loved him for that very reason. Over dinner Willow learnt what had been happening since she had been away. Thomas was back at work and the new mechanic was working out well.

"He's a decent young lad, Willow; I like him, and I think you should get to know him," hinted her father.

"It's alright Father, he's not really my type. I will find someone; I'm working on it," came the reply, not what he wanted to hear. Did this mean she had met someone in Australia while on holiday? Not ideal, but that would soon be forgotten because of the distance between them, her father smiled to himself.

A new season

TODAY IT WAS BACK to work, and Willow's beloved grapes were the first thing on her mind this morning. Ritchie had called last night and they had burbled love talk over the phone, and both had great holiday memories. She was happy that Alana's baby had not decided to come earlier as she was able to manage the irrigation and fertilising to ensure balanced growth. The nets had been removed by Thomas so now Willow had free access to the bulk of the crop. The harvesters were waiting on the go-ahead for the rest of the crop to be collected. The grapes had evenly turned from green to a translucent colour so now it was time to manually taste as well as use a refractometer to test them. The sugar levels had increased and the acidity had decreased so the flavours had developed enough to let Thomas and Steve know to start the following morning. It was later in the afternoon when she had finished sampling from different spots around the vineyard that she made her way to the workshop. On entering she found James sitting on Thomas's knee crying.

"What is wrong my darling, James?" she asked.

"The kids at school teased me when I told them I had a mother, and she lived in photos on the walls, she is just not here."

On hearing this, she had to hide her tears.

"Oh, James, we know Briar will always be with us in photos and most dearly in our hearts, so don't listen to their silly talk. We know better, don't we?"

Thomas was clearly upset seeing his son so unhappy, so the next day after he finished harvesting at 2pm he would take time out and visit the school and let them know what was happening.

Steve had been listening to the conversation and was surprised by the show of compassion coming from Willow. He had found her quite unapproachable and cold, so he had kept his distance from her. What he witnessed today gave him a little encouragement; perhaps she wasn't what he imagined. He had thought he might have asked her out one day, but then decided against it, but maybe that might change. She didn't seem to be attached to anyone, so a little more courage was what was needed. Willow's father had the same thoughts; he wanted her to find someone as she was getting older. He decided he would invite Thomas and Steve for dinner one night to see if any headway could be made in Steve's direction. He thought Steve would be a great catch, as it would be a partnership within the vineyard. He would work on it!

Willow was up at 5am and down at the winery to

oversee all was going well as the grapes were being brought in. The laboratory team were all there for the crushing, breaking the grape skins to release juice while avoiding excessive tannins from stems and seeds. These had to be removed while making white wine, to prevent any bitterness. The team also were responsible for fermentation temperature control and managing residual sugar, to balance sweetness and dryness. Then came the filtering, straining the wine to remove any remaining solids. Several other processes followed, and Willow's big part came creating the flavours commenced. This was the combining of wines from different grape varieties to achieve the desired taste. Tasting at every stage constantly was necessary in assessing the wines' development. This is where it was won or lost!

The harvesting was coming to an end; all the grapes had been removed and were now in liquid form in huge vats. Willow couldn't believe that all this time had passed, and she hadn't seen Ritchie. His embezzlement case was taking longer than he would have liked, so neither could leave their jobs. Now that things were slowing down a little it was time for her father to invite Thomas and Steve for dinner.

Willow wasn't told of these arrangements for fear she might opt out. This way it would be a surprise, a pleasant one her father hoped. As they came up the pathway Willow wondered if something had happened at the workshop, until she saw they were not wearing their work clothes. Her father invited them into the conservatory where there were a couple bottles of wine and glasses on the occasional table, along with some nibbles.

"What's going on here, are we celebrating something?"

"No, this is just a social drink," replied her father, "But we would like you and your mother's company. Come and join us."

With this, James appeared and as soon as he saw his father he rushed up to him and sat on his knee. He had formed a strong bond with him, and he wasn't about to let anyone change this. He at last had someone stable to call his own. He had asked Thomas when he could live with him fulltime, but no definite answer had been given, although one day soon a decision would have to be made.

The talk centred around the harvesting and how they thought the wine would turn out, whether there was an award to be won and who was going to be the kingpin, father or daughter. The family had not held their pre-season harvest party since Briar's death, as they still could not celebrate without their daughter and sister, and her death was still raw in their hearts. Alana and Timothy could not make it tonight as she was heavy into her pregnancy so just wanted to be at home.

Steve looked across at Willow; he liked what he saw tonight as she was chatty and happy, which made him think he could get to know her a little better. If he was confident enough, he might ask her if she would like to go on a date with him, but he would see how he felt at the end of the night. Willow's mother let them know that dinner was ready, so they made their way to the dining room. Her father made sure she sat next to Steve.

Conversation seemed to flow freely between them and this was observed by the head of the house. After dinner they went to the lounge to have a nightcap. Now was the time to call Thomas aside and leave Willow and Steve together.

"Do you like the vineyard work?" she asked.

Steve said he loved it; it was all new to him, but he found it interesting. Neither one spoke for a moment; was it now time to ask?

"Would you like to come out with me, Willow?"

She looked at him and told him she was already taken.

"Oh, I haven't seen you with a partner, so I thought you were available," he replied.

No, my man lives in Auckland and we don't see each other very much but we talk on the phone most nights. I'm sorry, Steve."

"You don't need to be sorry, that's okay," he answered in a disappointed voice. They talked until her father and Thomas returned. It was then Steve stood up and thanked his hosts for a lovely evening as he was taking his leave.

After the guests left, Willow's father asked her what she thought of Steve.

"He seems a nice young man. He asked me out on a date, but I told him I already had a boyfriend."

"But that's not true, Willow," said her father.

"I'm sorry, Father, but it is true."

With this he enquired as to who the boyfriend was. She cringed; how was he going to accept the next bit of news? It had to come out sooner or later, so now was the time. "I went to Melbourne with Ritchie; we are an item."

"You what … I don't like him Willow, he's not to be trusted."

"I'm sorry, Father, I happen to like him very much. What have you got against him?"

Would he tell her? No, it wasn't the right time, and she would be argumentative with him, but he was bitterly disappointed with her choice of a partner. Surely, she could do better than him? She had had years to sort out a decent man, and yet she had picked Ritchie. He did wonder if Ritchie had made advances and she had succumbed to them. This was the type of guy he was protecting his daughters against, and yet the smartest one had fallen for one.

His thoughts went back to Briar, and tears began to form. She had loved Thomas and from this love came James. The burning question was whether he would have been in favour of this relationship. He felt lost, as he missed her most of all. A part of him had died with her.

A new challenge to face

WILLOW'S immediate problem lay not with the vineyard but with Ritchie, as he was coming down to spend a week with her. They hadn't seen each other since their Melbourne getaway. He had arranged to stay with Timothy and Alana, so that alleviated one problem, but she did wonder how her father was going to react towards him. Of course, she had no idea her father had seen Kate and Ritchie undressing in the garden at Alana's wedding. He had not let go of this image so held it against Ritchie. He was not a guy he wanted any of his daughters to be associated with.

Willow was excited about him coming to stay, but she would have liked to have asked him to stay with her, to share her bedroom, but her gut feeling told her otherwise. Perhaps she could share his bed at Alana and Timothy's home; other than that there was always the lounge in the winery! Whatever her decision, it was bound to cause controversy with her father, and as yet her mother hadn't voiced her opinion.

Ritchie was flying into Blenheim at 6.30pm so Willow drove to the airport after work to be in plenty of time. She was so excited; she couldn't wait to be in his arms. She saw the plane approaching so walked to the huge window to watch him get off the aircraft. There he was walking across the tarmac, the handsome guy that he was. She had to pinch herself to see if this was really happening; was he her man? As he met her in the waiting area, he greeted her with a big wink and then she ran into his arms.

"Oh, I have missed you so much, Ritchie. Have you missed me?"

"Of course I have, you daft girl. I wouldn't be here if I didn't, as I had another proposal I could have kept."

Willow was quick to pick up on this so asked him what he meant.

"You know that well-known media person who was at our table in Melbourne, she emailed me to say she was coming to Auckland and would like to meet up with me."

"What a cheek," answered Willow.

"That's what happens when you are popular," he replied with a laugh. They picked up his luggage and headed to the car.

As they were driving home, Willow received a call to say Alana had gone into labour and Timothy was taking her to the hospital. Jessica was staying with their parents. This meant the house was theirs for at least one night. When they arrived, there was a note on the table to tell Ritchie to make himself at home. They took his bag to his room, and both fell onto the bed. They looked at each other and off came their clothes and under the bedclothes they dived. It was so good to be in each other's arms again. Willow had missed that wonderful feeling that not even her beloved grapes could give her, because before she met Ritchie, she didn't even know these feelings existed. His hands caressed her body, and he was a good lover, taking care to make sure Willow was sexually aroused before he satisfied himself. He was the complete package, and she was proud that she had saved herself for him. She didn't know how she had lasted so long without his body close to hers, but in a week's time he would be gone, and that loneliness would be there again. She switched off from this thought he was here now, and she would enjoy every moment. They would make love many times before Ritchie departed.

Willow spent the night in Ritchie's bed, and now morning had arrived, she dressed and made her way home. Just as she was coming in the door, she met her father.

"You're up early," he greeted her, knowing full well where she had been. Willow decided to bring things out in the open.

"Father, I hope you will be pleasant to Ritchie as it would make things easier for me. I love him, so please give him time to prove himself. He is coming down to the winery later; I'd like to ask you to make him welcome."

Her father looked at her and wondered why she couldn't see through him. Surely if he gave Ritchie enough time, he would hang himself.

"I will be polite, but I can't say I'm happy about the whole affair," he spoke his truth. Willow thanked her father.

Today was another wine-tasting day, and Willow had to get the right balance and blends of wine for that award-winning vintage. She was determined to win the top award this season, as now she was not a newcomer to the industry, so she was competing against experienced winemakers. She was up in the laboratory with the scientists watching as they added and subtracted small elements of the wine, tweaking where they thought necessary, but the final say was up to her; she was the winemaker. She was looking out for Ritchie to arrive as she wanted his input. She thought he was a very good entrepreneur so maybe his tastebuds were of help to her. Willow watched from above at her father working on the ground level; would he spot Ritchie before her, and could she rely on him keeping his word to make him feel welcome? If he got a wrong feeling about something, he was a hard man to convince otherwise. She felt nervous. Suddenly Ritchie appeared on the bottom level by her father, so she rushed down the stairs hoping to be there in time to whip him upstairs. Too late, she saw him shaking her father's hand.

"Nice to meet you again, boss," he greeted her father.

Willow stood and watched to see what happened next, as the two men stood and looked at each other. It was time to make her presence felt.

"Hi, Ritchie, I've been waiting for you so we could taste the new season's award-winning wine."

"I'm on for that," he replied. "Looks like I'm needed elsewhere. Please excuse us." With this he followed Willow up the staircase. Yes, he certainly had the gift of the gab concluded her father, but surely Willow would see he wasn't her type of guy!

The laboratory team had some vials of wine sitting on a shelf, all at different stages of fermentation. Now it was up to Willow to taste and see which one she liked most. This was where Ritchie came in. The vials were numbered from 1 to 12 so she asked Ritchie to write down what he gave each one out of ten. She would do the same then they could compare scores. The game was on but they were not allowed to talk while they were tasting. Thirty minutes went by, and now it was time to compare their scores. One of the laboratory staff looked on as they discussed each vial and what number it was given. To Willow's surprise neither had given a score of 10 out of 10, thus pointing to the fact that the award-winning wine had not yet been produced. They were close on several numbers but that was not good enough, and tomorrow was another day. There was still some mixing of varieties to hit the jackpot. The sweetness was still too high; they were looking for the perfect Sauvignon Blanc so the sweetness needed to be taken down a step.

Alana had still not had her baby, so Timothy was staying at the hospital with her, which meant they would have another night to themselves. They had been invited to Willow's parents for dinner and she had accepted, as she felt the barrier between her father and Ritchie could be softened. It was a rushed shower, a quick change of clothes by Ritchie, then he was meeting Willow at the parents' home. He didn't know that Willow's father had something against him; he just thought he didn't come across as particularly friendly probably because he didn't want to lose his daughter … a father–daughter thing. He was looking forward to catching up with James as he had taken a liking to him. As soon as James saw Ritchie he asked, "Will you come and play ball with me like last time?" So, the two went off together into the garden.

"I haven't seen you for a long time, Ritchie; where have you been?" Ritchie explained to James that he lived in Auckland and that was a long way from Blenheim.

"Are you Willow's boyfriend?" he asked. "Why don't you come and live with us?"

"Perhaps I might one day."

This seemed to satisfy James as he had no more questions. They kicked the ball around and laughed together, which drew Willow's father to see what was going on. He stood in the shadows of the veranda posts and watched as they were having fun. This surprised him as he never imagined Ritchie to even be interested in James. He retreated inside and had a little think to himself.

Willow was playing house with Jessica when she was called into the conservatory for a pre-dinner drink. Ritchie chose to sit next to Willow and of course James was right behind.

"One day Willow, Ritchie is coming to live with us, aren't you, Ritchie?"

This stopped any conversation dead in its tracks.

Willow looked blankly at James and asked why he had said that.

"Ritchie told me he was your boyfriend, so I asked him to come and live here with us."

This lightened the air a little. She could almost hear a sigh of relief coming from her father, who was now upright in his chair.

"You are a little matchmaker, James," remarked Ritchie.

This eased the situation a little further, although the distasteful look on her father's face told another story.

"How is your wine coming along?" he asked Willow, wanting to divert conversation away from any more romantic questions floating around in James's head.

"No, we are not quite there yet. Close, but not close enough, so hopefully tomorrow might yield some good news."

Willow's father was hoping to produce an award-winning Pinot Noir. His red wine was a later production than Willow's white wine.

The next question from Willow's father was directed at Ritchie. "What does your job entail at the law office?"

Ritchie explained that at the moment he was working on a huge embezzlement case, and it was taking longer than first anticipated, as an employee had stolen millions from a reputable firm and now it had overseas connotations. The employee had been escorted out of the premises before valuable information could be interfered with. A complaint was first filed with the police but now US federal authorities were brought aboard as it had extended across international borders, with money laundering part of it. Bank accounts had been frozen, and all property seized. Now it looked like it was going to end up as a public trial, because it was a reputational risk to the company.

"Is it nearing the end?" he asked.

Ritchie didn't know as now that it was a public trial new dates had to be arranged, but they could be months away.

"Do you have to be there until the end of the case?" Willow's father asked, hoping it would go on forever, so as to keep him away from his daughter. Still Ritchie hadn't cottoned on to the fact that Willow's father was trying to drive them apart. But Willow sensed this and was upset with her father; he was being subtle in a sarcastic way, but she could read the signs.

The children were put to bed and Willow and Ritchie stacked the dishes in the dishwasher and turned it on. It was getting late and Willow wanted Ritchie to herself, so they thanked the parents and left. As they walked back to Alana and Tomothy's home, Ritchie told Willow he found it hard to warm to her father.

"I'm sorry you feel like that, Ritchie. I think it is because he doesn't want to lose me, so he is being protective." What else could she say! She wished she knew why he didn't like him; perhaps she would ask him tomorrow at the winery. Tonight, they had the home to themselves again, so it was a race to the bathroom, which Willow won. She undressed to take a shower then called for Ritchie, who waltzed in naked, so she knew what was on his mind. They climbed into the shower together lathering each other's bodies, caressing and touching. Willow teased him by soaping his manly part and hiding it among the suds, and in retaliation he soaped her breasts, This brought playful laughter, the shower was turned off and two bodies collapsed to the shower floor. Legs went everywhere as they made love in such a confined space; it wasn't very comfortable but it was fun.

At some ungodly hour they were woken by the phone ringing. Willow jumped out of bed to answer, and there was Timothy's voice. She felt uncomfortable as she didn't know if he was happy with her being in his home.

"Hi, Timothy, you must have some news?"

"Yes, we have a baby daughter. Alana is exhausted and is thankful it is all over. Last one, she said, so looks like we are a four-person family."

"That's wonderful news. Give her our love and we will see you soon. Bye."

Willow jumped back into bed and put her cold feet on Ritchie's back. Wrong thing to do as this brought him to life and he cuddled hard into her.

"No, Ritchie, I need some sleep," she protested, but the protest was short lived.

They woke to a voice calling them, and there was Timothy standing at the end of the bed. Willow pulled the duvet over her head to hide and left Ritchie to explain.

"What happened in the bathroom last night? Your clothes are all over the floor, Willow, and there are bubbles everywhere."

"Oh my God" was heard coming from under the bedclothes.

"Sorry, bro, we will clean it up. What is the time?" Ritchie asked.

When they heard it was 10.30 Willow jumped up in bed but then dived down again, as she forgot she was totally naked. She should have been at work.

"Can you go, Timothy, so I can get dressed? I'm meant to be at work," she asked politely. She jumped out of bed and wrapped a towel around her and ran to the bathroom. Timothy was right; it was a right old mess. She picked up her clothes and dressed, then did a quick tidy-up; the rest Ritchie could do. As she passed Timothy on the way out, she apologised.

"It must have been some night," he remarked.

This sounded strange coming from him as he was a quiet person and quite boring she thought, unlike his brother.

She returned home to have a shower and get a change of clothes. There was no time for breakfast as she had to get to work. As she entered the winery, she was greeted by her father.

"I hope you are not just of bed, my girl?"

She was hurt by his remark so decided to ask him why he didn't like Ritchie.

"It is embarrassing for me, Father. What has he done to you to make you feel this way about him?"

Was now the right time to tell her? Yes, she asked so he let it all out.

"The day of Alana's wedding, no it was the nighttime while we were partying, I followed Ritchie and Kate into the garden and saw them undressing behind the bushes. I don't know what happened next because I left, but I was not impressed. He took advantage of an unsober person, and they had only met that day, so in my eyes he's a philandering egotistical guy who is out for a good time."

"Father, that was four years ago; he has changed. Remember he lived with Kate for three years," explained Willow.

"Then why did he drop her?"

"Because he liked me, so he didn't want to string her along. I didn't know this then." "Well, he has got to prove himself to me before I can accept him. I would prefer you chose Steve; he's a decent young man."

"Father, you can't choose for me. Steve is not my type of guy, and frankly I find him boring. Ritchie is a go-ahead and exciting person; that's why I like him."

"Your choice, not mine," said her father as he walked away.

This didn't help her one little bit.

Ritchie turned up at 12.30 with some lunch for Willow. They were sitting in the staff cafeteria eating when Willow's father walked in.

"Hi, Ritchie, I'm driving into town soon. Would you like to come with me?" he asked.

This took him by surprise, "Yes, that will be great," he replied.

Willow felt dubious about this. Why would he offer to take Ritchie with him, and what was he going to say? This left her feeling worried. She would just have to wait until they returned, then she would ask. The afternoon dragged as she kept wondering what was going on between her father and Ritchie. She wasn't in the mood to taste any wines, so put them on hold until the next day. She left the winery and drove towards the workshop. James was just coming down the road off the school bus, so she stopped and waited on him.

"Hi, my darling James, how was school today?"

"Do you know the holidays start tomorrow and I can't wait to go to my father's house. We both like talking to Briar as we love her. I'm happy I've got a father, but it will be better when I can live with him all the time. He is lonely without me. Grandad and Grandmother have each other, you have Ritchie, but Thomas has no one. Willow was nearly in tears. She had heard her parents talking and they didn't want to give James up, as they feel Briar's presence in him. They had been stalling on a decision. They had even been to a solicitor to find out who has the legal right to his guardianship. Sadly, they learnt the father was the legal guardian unless he was deemed unfit to care for him.

On hearing James's comments, she would bat for him to live with his father. Her parents would see him each day as he would still come home on the bus to Thomas's workplace. They weren't going to lose him totally. As they pulled up at the workshop, James jumped out of the car to go and see his father and give him a cuddle. She watched on and saw the love they had for each other. Yes, they definitely needed to be together.

James and Thomas

As the school bus let James off, he skipped along the road as tonight he was going home with his father, to stay for the school holidays. He had waited for what seemed a lifetime for these holidays to arrive. Tomorrow was the weekend, so he didn't need to come to the workshop as his father had the weekend off and they would be together. Little did he know his grandfather had invited them all for a family dinner as Alana had just come home today with their new baby.

James arrived at the workshop, and the first thing he did every day was give his father a big hug. Since Willow had witnessed this, she was determined to speak with her family about the relationship between James and his father. James desperately wanted to be with him, but the family were reluctant to let him go, even to the extent of finding out if they could become his legal guardians. Thomas would be shocked if he knew this had happened.

He felt he had been very fair letting James live with them as long as he had, but now was the time for him to bring him home. Thomas spent hours in front of Briar's photos shedding tears and telling her he loved her. Now was the time for him to have his son living in this home where he rightfully belonged.

"What time are you finishing tonight, Father?" James asked, as he couldn't wait much longer.

"We have been asked by your grandparents to stay for dinner tonight, as Aunty Alana is bringing her new baby for us all to see."

His lip went down, and he reluctantly said, "Oh, okay, I suppose we have to stay to see her, but I really wanted to go and talk to Briar."

"Never mind, we can do that later. We will leave straight after we have eaten," answered his father, who was also a little disappointed.

The drinks had started, so everyone raised their glass to wet the baby's head. As yet she didn't have a name. Jessica wanted to call her Amber, but this hadn't been finalised. The head of the family gave his speech,

"Welcome little one to your new family. It is lovely to have another younger generation joining us, and may there be many more ..." But before he could finish, Alana let him know she was not contributing further to extend the family; it was now up to Willow and Ritchie. This did not go down well; Willow noticed her father's face drop.

"Yes, you and Ritchie can have babies, then it will be a bigger family," piped up James. The conversation quickly changed back to the vineyard. If anyone could innocently upset the mood, it was James. He just said what came into his head at that moment in time.

Ritchie had not discussed with Willow what her father and him had talked about on their trip to town, but there was definitely tension between them. As much as she begged him to tell her, he remained tight lipped. If she knew she would be horrified, and he didn't want the family to fall apart. Ritchie had met his match, but he wasn't about to give in. He loved Willow and, in the end, if she had to make a choice, he felt confident she would choose him over her father, although there was a strong family bond.

Timothy nursed the baby most of the night as he never participated in the drinking scene. The family always celebrated important events with their wine, and it was a family tradition, but he had not become part of that culture, which at times made it hard for Alana when she felt like letting her hair down. She was not drinking tonight as she was breast feeding, but she took part in the celebrations. Timothy was a bit of a disappointment to the family as he tended to shy away from engagements, but Alana seemed to be happy; he was her choice!

James was starting to get a little restless, so Ritchie took him outside to kick the ball around.

"I just want to go home with my father," he told Ritchie. They were called in to eat so to the table they went. Dinner was a long, drawn-out process and James started to nod off.

"Come, James, I will put you to bed, and your father

can pick you up in the morning," said his grandfather. Thus began a scene no one saw coming.

"I don't want to stay here tonight. I'm going home with my father so we can sit and talk to Briar. She is my mother, and I love her just like Thomas. We both miss her, and she needs us to be there; we are her family."

This brought the room to a standstill; James had never talked like this before.

Now it was time for Willow to intervene.

"It's okay, James, you can go home with your father tonight. I know you want to live with him forever and that's fine. You, Thomas and Briar are a family so you should be together. I see how much you miss him; it is time for us to let go."

Her parents were in disbelief at what they had just heard. James was their only connection to their deceased daughter; his place was with them.

"Please stay out of this, Willow. It is nothing to do with you," said her father.

"But it is. I have seen the love between James and Thomas. Every day when they meet, he runs to him for his cuddle. He told me he wants to live with his father because he thinks he is lonely on his own. Please Father, can't you see this? You and Mother have to let go. This is James's life, not yours."

"Leave this home, Willow, and take Ritchie with you. You have said enough tonight."

"I'm sorry, Father, I can see you are hurt but look around and open your eyes as to what is happening here.

Come, Ritchie, we are leaving," and with this they thanked everyone.

"Don't go!" cried James, "I love you, Willow."

This was the time to take James home as he was clearly upset. What started off as a celebration ended in disaster.

Timothy could see what was happening and tried to calm the situation.

"Willow was right with what she said. James wants to look after his father, as he has no one else."

"But he is our connection to Briar, the only link we have left with her," argued his father-in-law father.

"But you must remember Briar chose Thomas; they loved each other. Imagine his grief at losing her. He needs their son."

With this Willow's father left the room. He just could not accept this. He loved Briar too, and she was his favourite daughter, but no one seemed to understand! With this, Timothy and Alana and their family said goodnight and left. On the way home Alana told Timothy he should not have intervened as it was not his business to become involved in.

"I had my say because Willow was right. I admire her for standing up to your father. He has to understand he is not the only one who misses Briar; we all do. But imagine how Thomas feels. We have all forgotten about his feelings, and he would have missed her more than all of us. Your parents have to let go."

When they arrived home, Willow and Ritchie were sitting having a coffee.

"Well, that went well," Timothy said to Willow.

"I'm sorry if I spoke out of turn, but I see how much James loves Thomas, and all he wants to do is look after him. Father and Mother have to let go or he will end up alienating himself from them. We all love James so we must do our best by him," she said convincingly. Alana sat quietly, upset the way the night had ended.

"I just want everyone to be happy," she said.

"But if Father doesn't let go, no one will be happy," Willow said. With this, Alana excused herself to tend to her baby. She was tired as it had been a long day.

Willow and Ritchie were a bit upset as they climbed into bed, so tonight cuddles were all that was happening in their bed. Willow lay there thinking about what her father had said. She had a restless night as the new baby made its presence felt. This made her think it wasn't the right time to be staying with Alana and Timothy with a newborn just home, so she would speak to Ritchie about getting a motel for the next couple of nights. She didn't think it was the right time to take Ritchie to her home to share her bed, not the way her father was at the present.

At the breakfast table she told Alana they were moving to a motel, She protested, but Willow explained that they should have their home to themselves when trying to settle a new baby in.

Meanwhile Thomas drove James home and he fell asleep in the car, so when they arrived, he lifted him out and took him inside and straight to his bedroom. He then pulled off his shoes and lay him under the bedclothes, and all the time he slept on. On reflection he was not happy with his boss, for if it wasn't for Willow stepping in, James would have slept at his grandparents' home. He had never seen his son so worked up and his outburst was heart-wrenching. Hence, he made the decision that James would not be going back to live with his grandparents; this was going to be his home from this day forth. He went to his favourite photo of Briar and kissed her goodnight and let her know that they were a family once again.

Over the weekend James and his father had a lot of fun: they spent time at the local park kicking the ball, they went to McDonald's for tea, and they sat at nights talking to and about Briar. At this stage of his life, he didn't understand the sad set-up between his parents, but one day he would have to be told. Tomorrow it was back to work for Thomas, and he was not looking forward to telling his boss that James would not be coming back to stay, that his home was with him. He had discussed it with James, and he was so excited to think he was going to live with his father forever.

Today both James and Thomas drove to work, as during the holidays he would have to come to the workshop each day with his father, but that was okay because he could see his grandparents and play with Jessica and see the new baby. Thomas arranged with his boss to come to his home after work as he wanted to discuss something with him. He was on edge all day as he knew this was going to be a touchy subject, as once his boss got something in his head, he was hard to convince otherwise, but he would stand firm. He didn't see much of James during his work hours as he was busy entertaining everyone, especially his grandparents. Now that he didn't have to live with them, he was happy to visit them.

As Thomas made his way to meet up with the grandparents, he felt uneasy; how were they going to react? They sat down in the conservatory without James as this was adult talk. Thomas started. "I have come here to tell you that James is staying on with me after the holidays. We have talked about it and he wants to live with me. I know this is not what you wanted to hear, but as his legal guardian I have the final say. I'm truly grateful for all your support in bringing James up; you have done a wonderful job, but now as his father it is my time to care for him."

His boss could not believe what he was hearing; this was his grandson, Briar's flesh and blood, who belonged with them. He stood up and walked around in circles wondering what to say to Thomas. He was furious. His wife asked him to sit down.

"I can't believe you would do this to us, Thomas; he is our grandson," she said.

"I realise that, but he is also my son, and I have a duty to Briar to care for him, as he is our child, he was born out of our love. You are not going to lose him; you will see him every day when he gets off the school bus, but it is my place to care for him."

There was silence.

Suddenly James appeared and saw them all sitting staring at each other.

"Isn't it great that I am going to live with my father

every day, but don't worry I can still see you. I'm so happy."

He looked around and then asked what was wrong as no one spoke.

"I have just told your grandparents that you are going to live with me, and they are very sad," Thomas said.

"Don't be sad. I'm happy," said an excited little boy.

There was nothing more to say, and the room stayed silent, so Thomas told James to get all the stuff he needed to take with him.

"Just drop his clothes into the workshop when you're ready. I would like to thank you once again for looking after James. He loves you both," he said, looking at James's grandmother.

As Thomas left with James, his boss was angry. "Who does he think he is just walking in and telling us that he was taking James from us? He won't be working here any longer," he said in anger.

His wife told him to calm down and to forget the thought of sacking him as then they might never see James again. At least they could keep an eye on him as he visited them each day after school. They knew they couldn't fight for custody as Thomas's name was on the birth certificate, so he was his legal guardian. Their solicitor had told them this when they enquired about guardianship.

Willow and Ritchie had moved into a motel at Renwick for their last two days. She hadn't told her father. They arrived at the winery to see how her wine was progressing. She knew producing a good wine was a blend of science, art and meticulous attention throughout the entire process. It was in her blood to compete alongside her father as he had years of experience. She hadn't seen him today, so she didn't know what the atmosphere was going to be. The laboratory staff were all given instructions as to the overall character, aroma, flavour and texture she was looking for, so each day she would come in and carry out the quality test. The wine lab was integral to crafting wines as they have to also make sure the wine is safe to drink and meets the highest quality standards. It was vital to reflect the winemaker's vision of an award-winning wine. This was her passion and her award to win. Ritchie was right behind her; he was enjoying learning about producing wine. When the wine was ready to be sold, he would promote it around the law fraternity in Auckland; he was a good salesperson as Willow had found out. That was where it all started with her and Ritchie, at the People's Choice award night the previous year.

Today was D-Day. The final decision on the finished product, and Ritchie's farewell. Last night very little sleep was had, as they didn't know when their next meeting would be, but lasting memories would keep them close … in all an exhausting but wonderful night. Ritchie's flight wasn't until 4.30pm so he came to the winery with Willow. As they entered, they were met by her father who seemed a little aloof towards them.

"Ritchie flies out today, Father, so I will drive him to the airport at 3.30. We are here to do our final tasting, then it will be in the lap of the gods. I hope they will be kind to me this year," she concluded.

She waited for her father to respond. All he could manage was "Good luck".

"What is wrong with you? I know I upset you when I agreed that James should live with his father, but we cannot go on like this. We were once a happy family but that is changing; why!"

"I lost a daughter, and her son is my only connection to her I have left. He must live with us. Now you and Ritchie, this is not what I wanted for you, Willow. I chose a nice young man in Steve, and you have just ignored him."

"Well, I'm sorry, Father that you don't agree with my choice of a partner, but you will just have to get used to it, as it will not go away. But James you can see every day when he gets off the school bus, so you are not losing him, and he loves you and Mother. Let go of him and he will always be part of your life."

After listening to these words, he departed with a quick "Goodbye, Ritchie," which went against his grain. What on earth did his intelligent daughter see in this flamboyant untrustworthy guy?

Headlines!

FOUR MONTHS HAD PASSED, and the wine awards were to be announced next week. Willow was thrilled with her vintage but was sad because Ritchie couldn't attend as his embezzlement case was before the court. Because of the complexity of the missing money, it was now worldwide news, as many countries were involved. Media from around the countries involved, including Australia, were there every day reporting the events. Ritchie was being harassed by the high-profile media lady they had sat with at the wine awards in Melbourne; she would not let go. She was at each hearing so of course they came in contact each day. She tried hard to lure him into a situation that would compromise his relationship with Willow, and at times it was a temptation as she was a very attractive woman, but his feelings for Willow won out. She knew he had a partner and tried to bribe him by saying that it would be kept a secret between them, but, no, he knew the consequences.

Willow and her family were following the case each night on the news, and tonight there was a live picture of Ritchie being interviewed by an Australian news reporter.

"Oh my God," exclaimed Willow.

"What's wrong, Willow? Do you know her?" asked her mother.

"She came on to Ritchie when we were in Melbourne at the wine awards, and she even slipped a note into his pocket arranging to meet him."

This was her father's opportunity to score handsomely.

"I told you he wasn't to be trusted. He's a predator looking for an easy ride to take him through life, and he found you. Open your eyes, my girl, he will hurt you. Steve is still waiting; he is a decent young man."

With these comments ringing in her ear, she left the room with her cell phone. She just had to call him to make sure there was nothing going on. She knew within her heart he wouldn't let her down, but she had to have his reassurance.

"Hi, my darling, how did the awards go?" he asked.

"Ritchie, I have just seen you on TV talking to that media woman from Australia. I hope you are staying true to me." She sounded upset.

"Do you think I would compromise our relationship for a one-night stand with her. I'm not interested; she is, but she knows my position so, no, there are no worries in that department."

Willow felt relieved. She was sure she could trust him, but it was just her father's words that made her feel uneasy.

"By the way, the awards are on Saturday night, so wish me luck."

This gave Ritchie an idea: he would try to get a flight to Wellington then another one on to Blenheim for Saturday, stay the night and fly home on the Sunday. This would be a surprise for Willow. He would book a hotel room for them on the Saturday night then would turn up unannounced at the awards.

Back at home, Willow's father was sure the romance was all off, which he suspected would happen. He was obviously having an affair with the Aussie media lady. He knew Ritchie couldn't be trusted. Perhaps in future his head-strong daughter would listen to his words of wisdom. He had invited Steve to accompany them to the awards. Willow knew this and didn't mind as he was part of the team, driving the harvester along with Thomas, so, yes, he should be invited to attend.

The awards night had finally arrived, so everyone was dressed in all their finery. Not only were the wines on display but so were the competing winemakers. The men were in tuxedos and the women in their formal gowns or cocktail dresses. Both the girls looked stunning; it was a rare occasion for Alana to dress up for a night out. Timothy had elected to stay at home and look after the girls. The awards night wasn't his scene, but for the sisters it was a big event. Their father had instilled in them that this was a team effort to produce the final result. It was not achieved by one person alone.

The Pinot Noir was the first prize giving. Third place was announced first, then the runner-up then the top award. Willow's father waited in anticipation for his name to be called out. He wasn't third, or second, then the final announcement.

"Will Mr Morrisey please come forward and collect first prize. His Pinot is outstanding in taste, texture and presentation. Congratulations, sir," the judge announced. The family let out a loud burst of applause as he made his way up to collect the trophy. 'Speech, speech' was echoed around the room.

"Thank you, everyone, I am dedicating this to my deceased daughter, Briar. This is for you dear daughter, we miss you so much," he said among his tears.

As he was leaving the stage, his eye caught a figure standing at the back of the room. No, no it couldn't be, but, yes, there was Ritchie looking quite the part in his tuxedo. What was that bastard doing here? He would get to him before Willow saw him. Was he here to try to woo her back? Not on his watch.

"What are you doing here?" he demanded.

"I've come to support Willow tonight. This is a surprise visit, I'm just going to find her." "Oh no, you are not, I know your type. You're only here for the glamour and the rewards, so stay away from my daughter. I'm warning you," he said in a threatening manner.

"Mr Morrisey, if I told your daughter you offered to pay me off to disappear out of her life, how do you think she would feel? We love each other so no amount of threats or bribery will stop me from loving your daughter. Now let me pass." Willow's father stood directly in front of him, refusing to move.

Then suddenly came the announcement for the best Sauvignon Blanc. This stopped the two men in their tracks.

"Would Willow Morrisey please come up and accept her trophy. This looks like a family affair, two top prizes to the same winery. The name of your wine, Harvest of Hearts, sounds quite appropriate. Please tell us why you selected that name."

Willow was stunned. Secretly she wanted this to happen, but what a surprise.

"Thank you everyone, and a special thank you to my sister Alana and to all the staff at our winery as this was a team effort. To my deceased sister Briar, this is for you, you are forever in our hearts. This is why I named my wine Harvest of Hearts, because of the closeness of us three sisters; this is where our hearts belonged." This brought a loud applause from the crowd. Then she saw Ritchie.

"Oh, I have just seen my partner. He has been busy in Auckland; this is a surprise!" With this, Ritchie moved past Willow's father and met her on stage. He leaned over and kissed her on the cheek and everyone applauded. It was what happened next that brought the crowd to their feet. Ritchie got down on his knee and proposed to her. It didn't take long for Willow to say yes.

When they made their way back to where the family

and Steve were seated, Willow noticed her father was missing.

"Where is Father?" she asked. No one had seen him except Ritchie, but he wasn't about to say anything. Then came an announcement over the speaking system.

"Are there any medical personnel present? Would they come to the foyer immediately please?" Willow panicked. Did her father need help? She rushed to the foyer and found him slumped in a chair surrounded by people.

"Father, what happened?" she asked.

"That Ritchie pushed me over. He is no good for you, Willow. Ditch him – he's trouble."

"No, you're wrong, Father, he would never do that to you," she protested.

"It's either his word or mine, it's your choice."

Everyone was moved away because the ambulance had arrived to take him to hospital. What was she meant to believe? No, Ritchie wouldn't do that, but she hadn't heard his side of the story. She found her family and told them that their father was taken to hospital. Alana agreed to take them there and Steve took his leave. Willow got Ritchie aside and questioned him.

"Tell me the truth, what went on between you and Father?"

"Your father was angry when he saw me. He must have thought we were not together anymore. He said I was the wrong one for you and to go straight back to Auckland. I stood up to him and told him we were adults able to make our own minds up as to who we wanted to see. Then we heard your named being mentioned so I moved past him to catch a glimpse of you. I don't know what happened after that, that is my truth, Willow."

"I must get to the hospital with the family," she said.

Ritchie offer to drive her, but she refused. He handed her a card with the name of the hotel.

"I will wait for you," he said.

By the time the family reached the hospital the medical staff had found out what had happened. He had had a mild heart attack and would fully recover but needed to stay in hospital for a couple of days while they ran tests. He needed rest so was not allowed visitors. Alana drove their mother home while Willow took a taxi from the hospital to the hotel. A night of high expectations had emerged, but the result was devastating. They should have been celebrating instead of visiting a hospital. Her dream had come true, but the excitement hadn't happened, and on top of that was Ritchie's proposal; had it come at the expense of her father? As she walked into the foyer of the hotel, there was Ritchie waiting for her. The tears started, but where to from here? Did she have to make a choice?

The night was not what Ritchie had hoped for, tensions were high, and Willow was upset about her father. She had just won the award she had worked hard for, she had been proposed to, but she felt flat. What was happening? She should have been on top of the world. Ritchie took her in his arms and held her close.

"Nothing has to happen tonight. Let us just get into bed and lie together. You have had a lot going on today. Congratulations on winning the top award – you deserved it, and we will celebrate when you feel the time is right."

They climbed into bed and within minutes Willow was sound asleep. The next morning Ritchie was catching his flight back to Auckland as he had to be at the court first thing on Monday morning. Willow apologised for not being sociable the previous night, but Ritchie understood.

"Thank you for your proposal. I am so happy. You are the man I want to spend all my days with. Father will just have to get his head around this, otherwise he will lose us. He has lost Briar and he won't want to lose me as family means so much to him."

It was sad goodbyes once again!

Ritchie's embezzlement case was finally coming to a close and a verdict was not far away. Only a small amount of the embezzled money was accounted for, as it had been laundered overseas as well as through several casinos throughout the country. The path of the missing money had gone cold once it left New Zealand. Although the high-profile company had seized all the offender's assets, they fell well short of the amount of embezzled money. It was now up to the court to bring the perpetrator to justice.

Two years on

WILLOW AND RITCHIE had been married for two years. There had been many ups and downs, but love won out in the end. Theirs had been a quiet wedding as her father still held Ritchie responsible for his heart attack. They had bought a home in Blenheim and she drove out to the winery each day. Ritchie had opened a law office in Blenheim, a subsidiary of the Auckland office. The wounds had never healed between her father and Ritchie. She did think her father was unfair about their situation, but it was something that would take time to mend, if ever!

They had been desperately trying to have a family, but nothing was happening. In the end Willow decided to find out if there was any reason that she couldn't conceive. When the tests came back, they were dealt a devastating blow, as she was not able not fall pregnant. They were both terribly upset. They spent a lot of time with James, who was growing into a lovely boy, very affectionate, and who adored his father. Her father had not totally got over the fact that James wasn't living with them, but they did get to see him every weekday. He loved catching up with Jessica and her sister. Sometimes Alana would walk them up to feed the pigs. They were huge animals, but the little piglets were cute. When they were told that was where their bacon came from, James and Jessica screwed up their noses. Willow and Ritchie's lives weren't completely empty as they had the children around to keep them occupied.

Willow's father put her infertility down to her disobeying him. It was karma, as he didn't want her to have children with Ritchie. Steve was still available, and he hoped the marriage would break down so she could end up with him, but in reality this was not likely. It was time for her father to forgive and forget, but as head of the family, he still ruled with an iron fist.

Willow found herself drifting away from the family, as she loved Ritchie and felt he should have been accepted. Alana and Timothy were sad about the whole situation as they could see how it was affecting the family bond. James was the heart and the centre of the family, and they all loved him for who he represented, but also for himself, as he was a nice innocent kid. He kept them in stitches at times; you had to be careful what was said in front of him. This happened one day when he heard his grandfather and grandmother talking about Willow not having children. They hadn't told their family why. James overheard his grandfather telling his grandmother that he didn't want Willow to have children with Ritchie. He couldn't understand this, so he would ask Willow why. The day arrived when he brought the subject up with Willow and Ritchie.

"Why doesn't Grandad want you to have babies?"

"What do you mean?" asked Willow.

James told them what he had heard being talked about between his grandparents. "But you should have babies. You like Jessica and me," he said in all innocence. Willow was livid as was Ritchie. Why would they wish this on anyone, especially their own family?

Nothing was said about James's conversation as they didn't want him to get into conflict, so they let it lie. Willow didn't visit as much; she was devastated that her father could be so pig-headed. She knew that she had to work alongside him in the winery, so she chose not to make the conflict any worse. He had changed since Briar passed away, and it was almost as if he had lost himself, which was why he attached himself so closely to James. This meant any interference with James was a loss to him, and when she had suggested that he live with his father, his attitude changed towards her. But James's life was not theirs to live.

One weekend afternoon a police car pulled up outside Willow and Ritchie's home. An officer came to the door and asked if Ritchie Taylor lived there. Willow asked him to come in. Yes, Ritchie lived here.

"I'm Officer Jason. I don't know how to break this to you as I don't know your current situation, but I have some sad news. The police in Australia have contacted us to tell us there was a horrific attack, a home invasion, and a young woman has died. Her name was Kate Mitchell. You, Ritchie, have been named next of kin. Do you know her?" he asked.

They both sat in shock. What did they mean, a home invasion? What had happened? How did she die?

"Did she suffer?" Ritchie asked. The police officer could not say much about the attack. He was just told the basics.

"That is not all. She has left behind a son and your name was on the birth certificate as his father. The little boy has been put in welfare care until you collect him. I can leave you some details as to how to make contact with the relevant authorities."

Neither Ritchie nor Willow could talk; this was a terrible shock. First Kate dead and her little boy on his own with no one. Ritchie burst into tears. He had had no idea Kate was pregnant; why hadn't she told him? He knew she had loved him and when he broke up with her she was so upset, but perhaps she didn't know at that time?

"Oh my God, what have I done?" he sobbed. "I have a son I didn't know about, but Kate, she is gone. What a terrible thing to have happened to her. Did the little boy see what happened to his mother?"

So many questions, and no answers. The officer could see the trauma they were suffering, so didn't offer any details and excused himself.

It took what seemed like hours before the silence ended. It was such shocking news, and where would they start? The worst shock of all was Kate's death, and trying to comprehend how it happened, why it happened and who would do such a thing. Was she trying to protect her son when she was attacked? And the little boy, was he alright?

"I am devastated," Ritchie said, "I could have helped Kate with the maintenance of our son; did she struggle to bring him up? What age would he be?"

They tried to work out how long ago it was when they parted, then to add nine months on to that, which would make him between three and a half and four years old. Willow remembered several times Kate had to fly to Australia while looking after James to visit her sick mother. Perhaps they could take comfort in the fact she lived with her. This was a scenario like Briar's all over again: two friends whose lives were taken too soon.

Willow was still trying to calm Ritchie as his sobbing hadn't stopped. She put her arms around him and reassured him everything was going to be alright.

"We will have to get a flight to Australia as soon as possible and contact the authorities to find out the full story, and pick up our little boy," she whispered to him. It was so sad to think one person's sorrow was another person's joy. Ritchie couldn't believe that Willow was so accepting of the situation, but then Kate was not a stranger, she was once considered part of the Morrisey family. Also, she had lived with Ritchie for a few years so it wasn't just a brief affair, rather it was something that could have happened to anyone while living in a partnership.

A sudden departure

THEY BOTH DECIDED against telling the family for the time being. But everyone was puzzled by the quick trip to Australia.

Ritchie and Willow flew into Melbourne late at night and stayed in accommodation near the airport for convenience. The next day they were going to call into the police station that they were given the address for. All night they talked about what they were going to find out the next day. There was sadness as well as a little happiness; to think they were going to be parents to a little boy, Ritchie's own flesh and blood.

A taxi took them to the police station, and they had a contact name to ask for. They were shown to a room where they had to wait until the officer was available. Then something suddenly dawned on Ritchie: would they be able to bring the little one home without a passport? He wasn't sure what age they were allowed to fly on their parents' passports. Willow couldn't throw any light on this either. They waited until an officer walked through the door and introduced himself. He was appointed to the Katie Mitchell case, so he had all the information they required.

"How can I help you? Where do we start?" he asked.

"Can you please tell us what happened to Kate and was there a reason?" asked Ritchie.

The officer answered. "I will tell you what we know. A neighbour heard a little child crying so they went in to see what was wrong and that's when the body was discovered. Kate must have disturbed a burglar who fought with her and hit her over the head. It was the head injury that did the damage; she would have died instantly. The neighbours took the little boy to their place then rang the police. We did a search and found her drawers had been disturbed but we don't know what was missing. The little boy is in welfare care and is being well looked after. He is a happy little soul, and it looks like he was too young to sustain any mental hurt. He does keep asking for his mummy, not understanding that something happened to her and that she was not coming back. I believe you are the father. Will you be taking the little boy back to New Zealand?" he asked.

"We did worry about a passport," Ritchie said.

"No worries there, as we found two passports on a dresser. It was as if she was planning on going overseas, probably back to New Zealand."

This only added to Ritchie's heartache. Was she

bringing their baby back to see him? "Has my son a name?"

"Yes, he is called Mathew Taylor."

Ritchie couldn't hide his tears. Kate had given him his surname, not her own. He felt so bad; he had let her down and now she was gone.

They found out Kate's mother had died and left her the home, so she had somewhere to live. The burning question was what was going to happen to her body? "Can we bring her body back to New Zealand? I want our son to have somewhere to visit when he grows older. She has to be remembered."

The officer told him he would have to take that up with the authorities, but he didn't think it would be a problem.

"Can we visit Mathew now?" Willow asked.

The office offered to drive them to where Mathew was in care, so they accepted as Willow just wanted to hold the little soul and comfort him. Fancy going through all that trauma at such a young age. Her thoughts went back to James; why did children have to suffer?

They were introduced to the matron who ran the home. She told them he was a happy little boy but was still asking for his mummy, and asking was she still sleeping? So, he did have some recollection of the last moment he saw his mother. They were led to a nursery where several children were playing.

"Mathew, someone has come to see you," she called. With this a little boy with curly hair came up to them.

"Hello, Mathew, my name is Willow and this is Ritchie.

We are going to take you for a little holiday, would you like that?" she asked.

"Can my mummy come too?"

What could they say? The room went silent. It was the matron who came to the rescue.

"Mathew, you know your mummy was very sick and she has gone to live with the angels. These people are going to love you like your mother. In fact, this is your father. He wants you to come and live with him; won't that be good!" Mathew looked at Ritchie and went to him and shook his hand.

"Hello, Father," he said. "I have seen you in the photo." This brought Ritchie to tears, and he lifted the little boy up and sat him on his knee.

"Do you like kicking a ball?' he asked. Mathew nodded and smiled. The ice was broken. Ritchie was so happy; here was his son and he felt a love that he had never felt before.

There was a lot to attend to: the house had to be sold as Kate had no family, so Willow and Ritchie spent several days getting it ready for sale. In the main living area was a photo of Ritchie, which must have been the photo Mathew mentioned. It was while sorting out Kate's home that Ritchie felt remorse. He found more photos of him and Kate taken while they lived together. He wondered if he had not met Willow whether he and Kate would still have been together. If so, she would not have gone to Australia and would be still alive today. He remembered she was heartbroken when he told her he loved Willow. She had been hurt before and vowed never to let it happen again, but it did. This was when she decided to go to Australia. Her mother was not well so she would go home and look after her.

At that time, she had no idea she was pregnant. It wasn't until a few months later that she wasn't feeling well, so made an appointment to see a doctor. After he did tests, he confirmed that she was indeed pregnant. Her mother was happy at the thought of becoming a grandmother and having them both living with her. As Kate's time drew near her mother's health deteriorated and, sadly, she didn't live to see her grandchild. This left Kate on her own once again, and it brought back memories of her time with Briar and looking after James. She had loved her life while living with the Morrisey family. They had been happy times on the vineyard, and it was there she met Ritchie.

She never thought she would ever find love again, as she had loved before and had been badly hurt, so swore to herself it would never happen again. She still remembered the day they met; it was Alana and Timothy's wedding day. Well into the night after having had too many wines she and Ritchie went into the garden behind the bushes and in a lustful moment, they undressed each other and ended up having sex. From then on there was no going back for Kate; he had won her heart. He was good looking and very self-assured, and she felt he was definitely the one, and their relationship was going to be everlasting, but sadly Willow got in the way.

After having the baby, she did wonder if she should contact Ritchie and let him know they had a son, but time just seem to pass. She didn't have to go to work, perhaps not until Mathew started school, as her mother had left her the home and her invested money. This meant she could be a stay-at-home mum. She did not want another relationship; Mathew was her life, and she enjoyed watching him grow. She decided to enrol him in a child play group so he could meet other children. He was three and a half years old and had not interacted much with other children, so she wanted to prepare him for when he started school. He found it daunting at the start and begged his mother stay with him for the first few times. Then as he came out of his shell and got to know some of the children, he didn't need her to stay with him. Kate was pleased she had made that decision to integrate him into a classroom situation, where he could gain a little confidence and learn to mix and share with other children.

Then one day she decided she would like to visit New Zealand to see James and the Morrisey family so arranged for passports for them both. She hadn't decided if she would tell Ritchie about Mathew, that decision would be made later. The passports duly arrived, and now she could start planning for their holiday … and that's where it all ended.

Ritchie found the passports on the dresser in the bedroom. The police had seen them and taken notes. There were no brochures indicating where they might have been going for a holiday. He found plenty of toys and clothes in the spare room which showed him that Mathew had not gone without, a comforting thought for Ritchie.

In his heart he knew Kate would have been a good mother, as she was not afraid to share her feelings.

It was while going through her personal papers that Ritchie found an unopened envelope addressed to him. He held on to it, not knowing what to do, and turned it over several times before deciding to open it, in case there was something of importance he should know about. As he silently read the contents, he was heartbroken. Kate revealed her love for him and was writing the letter to let him know if anything happened to her, Mathew was to be brought up by him, as he was the love of her life. At that moment in time, he felt like a despicable sod who had totally ruined Kate's life. She had done nothing wrong; rather he was the one who had done wrong. She had been a loving partner, but his heart lay elsewhere. He wondered if she had thought of sending this to him, or it was only to be seen upon her death. Every day when he looked at Mathew he would be reminded of Kate; she deserved that at the least. He would always tell him that his mother loved him dearly, and he would never forget her.

This was where Willow found Ritchie, sitting on the floor by the cabinet sobbing his heart out, with the letter clutched in his hand. Willow sat down beside him, and she could see he was devastated. She took the letter from him and began reading it. The tears followed, as she felt she had been the cause of all this pain, because Ritchie loved her instead. Yet there was no going back; it had happened. But they made a promise to each other that no matter what, Kate would never be forgotten.

The clearing up continued. All Kate's clothes were in

her wardrobe and drawers, so Willow told Ritchie she would see to these items. She found jewellery at the bottom of a drawer, some of which would have been Kate's mother's so she put it all in a bag to take home with her, as one day in the future Mathew would meet someone and these would be family keepsakes.

Meanwhile Ritchie went next door to talk with the neighbour, to see if she could throw some light on what had happened. She said Kate was a good neighbour who kept pretty much to herself and loved her little boy. She would hear them out playing in the yard laughing together. What happened was a shocking tragedy. She heard Mathew crying for quite some time early in the morning, so she went over to see if he was okay, and it was then she discovered Kate's body lying on the floor. She was thankful no blood could be seen as Mathew thought Kate had fallen asleep. That was all he could remember. She brought him to her home and rang the police straight away to tell them what she had discovered. She wanted to look after Mathew, but she had a job and had to go to work, so the police said they would make sure he was looked after until the next of kin was contacted.

The police were trying to piece it all together as there seemed to be no motive for Kate's brutal murder. The only thing they could put it down to was she must have heard noises downstairs and was worried, so went to investigate and disturbed the intruders, who then picked up a rolling pin and hit her around the head with such force it damaged her brain, and she died instantly. It must have been after that they went upstairs and ransacked her drawers. The television was gone as were most other electronic items. Sadly no one saw anything untoward in the street that night, so the police had no leads. They would put as many police as they could spare on the case, as it was a horrific murder that needed to be solved. Other neighbours were worried that it might happen again, so the street was cordoned off. The police promised Ritchie they would indeed find the offenders and bring them to justice. Such a senseless brutal murder would not go unsolved; it would take priority.

After spending more days than they thought getting things sorted out, they called the Salvation Army to come and take everything from the inside of the home apart from some photos of Kate and Mathew together. These would be treasures dear to their hearts, as Kate had been a big part of both their lives. The proceeds of the house sale would be put into a bank account for Mathew. They had heard back from the authorities and, yes, it was fine for Kate's body to go back to New Zealand. There was a lot of red tape to go through, but Ritchie couldn't leave her body in Australia, not after what had happened to her.

First, there were strict biosecurity and legal requirements. They needed to appoint an Australian funeral director for paperwork, embalming and transportation logistics. A New Zealand funeral director had to receive the body, and this was followed by a death certificate, passport or identification and the airline documentation. The body had to be transported in a sealed approved casket. Once in New Zealand the

Ministry for Primary Industries had to be notified for biosecurity standards, then the casket was inspected by New Zealand Customs. It was going to cost a lot of money, but to Ritchie it had to be done this way for his son's sake. In years to come, he had to know where his mother was. Willow completely agreed with Ritchie's wishes.

Their stay in Australia was a little longer than planned as to get everything arranged took time. Every day they went to the home to visit Mathew, and he waited for them to arrive. A family bond was forming, and he was looking forward to his holiday.

At last, the day had arrived. Willow and Ritchie picked Mathew up from the home and left a large donation to express their gratitude for the kindness shown to their little boy. He didn't know he was flying in a big plane so was excited when he was told. He stayed awake for a couple of hours then fell off to sleep. Ritchie had to wake him to say they had arrived in New Zealand. The flight landed in Wellington. They had to wait for the funeral director to collect the casket, take it through Customs then put it on the flight to Blenheim where it would be met by another funeral director, who would keep it until a funeral was arranged.

Willow and Ritchie were worn out and they just wanted to get home with Mathew. Willow cuddled him on their flight to Blenheim as he was also tired. It had been a long day for them all. They couldn't get over how quickly Mathew had accepted them, and as yet he hadn't asked for his mother, but that would come!

Once settled in, Mathew seemed happy in his new environment. He did ask for his mother several times and was told she loved him but because she was sick she had gone to live with the angels. Now it was time to have a family meeting and explain their sudden departure to Australia. Willow asked Thomas to come to the meeting and bring James, as Kate had been a big part of their lives also. When they arrived everyone was there, and when they walked in with Mathew, all eyes focused on him. James was the first to speak.

"Who are you? What is your name?" he asked. "Do you kick a ball?" Mathew nodded. "Come out and play with me." The two boys left the room.

"Who is that dear little boy?" asked Alana.

Willow warned them what they were about to hear was going to be a shock. She relayed the whole story, which took everyone by surprise. They were upset to know that Kate had passed away under such tragic circumstances, but who was the little boy? Now it was Ritchie's story to tell.

"Mathew is my and Kate's son. I didn't know she was pregnant until a police officer called to tell us she had been attacked and had passed away. We have brought her body back and are going to have a proper funeral for her, so that Mathew knows where his mother is buried. I will arrange Kate's funeral tomorrow and will let you all know when it is going to be held.

There wasn't a dry eye in the room. Kate had been very much part of all their lives and now she was gone. It was as if it was happening all over again, first Briar and now Kate. Two young women in their prime leaving behind their sons who had to reconnect with their fathers. Willow watched her father; he was visibly upset. There had been so much sadness, so how was he going to handle this? Suddenly the peace was broken when two excited boys came bursting into the room, and the sadness seemed to slowly disappear. Here was life, the next generation, so full of energy and happiness.

"Guess what? I have a new friend, and he is living with his father, that's you, Ritchie, I knew you were a good father."

This comment from James was all it took to turn a sad home into a home with an outlook that would bring a little happiness in days to come.

Kate's funeral was a private affair, just for those that knew her. It was what she deserved. The children didn't attend because Mathew and James had been told their mothers had gone to live with the angels. They stayed behind with Timothy and the girls. When they were old enough to understand, they would be told the truth. At least Mathew now had somewhere to go in the future if he wanted time alone with his mother. Meanwhile that role would be filled by Willow, as she would love Mathew as her own. Was this the breaking of the ice between Ritchie and his father-in-law? He could see that everything that was needed to be done in the right manner had been handled with dignity, so was it time to bury the hatchet and make amends? They were all invited back to the winery after the funeral. Several bottles of wine were opened; what better way to remember Briar and Kate than at the place where so much had taken place?

At the end of the gathering as everyone was about to depart, Willow's father called Ritchie aside. He could see his daughter slowly drifting away from the family circle. He had already lost one daughter; he couldn't afford to lose another.

"It is about time I put aside my stubbornness and accepted you as my son-in-law. You have proved to me all I wanted in a family member, so let us shake hands and call a truce." With this he held out his hand, and Ritchie shook it. This was followed by a hug, and now hopefully there would be a friendship between them.

The vines were bursting into bud, signalling a new harvest was about to flourish. Alana had the nursery stocked with many native plants that she had cultivated from cuttings. This was her speciality. The waterways were looking clear and healthy, thanks to her plantings, which helped keep the pollutants away from streams. She took the girls there with her each day; it had become part of their life. Jessica had just started school so walked to the school bus stop and would come home in the bus each night with James, who was attending intermediate school now. First stop was always the workshop so James could see his father. . Mathew went to the same school as Jessica; his father dropped him off each day on his way to work. In a roundabout way the next generation were all cousins, and they stuck by each other, the vineyard being their homebase.

The spraying season was upon Alana once again, along

with the soil tests to see all the chemicals were balanced for the vines to thrive. Now with the little ones about, she had the chemicals under lock and key, as this was one of her main worries, she didn't want the authorities to come on to the property and find they weren't housed properly. Work & Safety were not an easy outfit to deal with, so better everything was in order, then there was no cause for them to visit the property.

James had reached the age to understand the complexity of the vineyard, so it was time to hold a family meeting on the subject of the 'family inheritance'. Being the eldest of the next generation, the title would be given to him. Secretly Willow's father was thrilled that Briar's legacy was the one to carry it on. Because the first born of Willow's generation were triplets, all three carried the 'Inheritance' title so they were the principal shareholders. When their reign ended James would take that position. It would be a challenge for him, but who better to carry it on? He was adored by every family member. With each generation came jubilation along with tribulations; it was a matter of the family bond continuing to stay strong.

The bond could have been broken if the head of the family hadn't conceded that he was out of order and that he could not pick who his daughters chose as their partners. Competition was still rife between father and daughter, and their success over the years had put their wines on the top shelves of many sales outlets along with the many trophies they both displayed.

Ten years on

Today things looked a lot different. Willow's father had retired due to health problems, so he had moved into Willow and Ritchie's home. Now Willow, Ritchie and Mathew were living in the family home on the vineyard. This worked out well for Mathew as he was closer to his cousins, and they were all at high school in Blenheim. As for James, he was in Adelaide at the college for viticulturists, as he had chosen to follow the family's path and become a winemaker.

Both James and Mathew had been told about their pasts, how their families evolved out of much sadness, but it was in the present that they chose to live.

Willow and Ritchie enjoyed their life together, but alas Timothy and Alana's relationship had fallen apart. When it was announced they were going to part the thought of a settlement between Alana and Timothy was a worry to her father as they could lose some of the equity in the vineyard as part of the settlement. But Timothy's beliefs didn't allow him to take from something that wasn't his. He insisted it belonged to Alana, it was her birthright, so this was a huge relief to the family. He had been paying off their home to her parents, so they had kept the money in a separate bank account. When it came to Timothy buying a home, he didn't have enough money, so his in-laws paid for it as their grandchildren were involved. They explained to him it was his own money they were giving back. It took a lot of persuasion but in the end, he had no choice but to accept it, for which he was grateful.

The family were sad it had come to this, but Alana's life was being compromised by Timothy's way of thinking. They would remain good friends which meant the girls weren't torn, as they had access to both parents. Timothy bought a home in Blenheim and they shared the girls. He could never accept that when presents were given, it was not a show of wealth as he perceived, but an act of kindness. He still loved Alana but because their values and lifestyles were so different, and as much as he did try, it all became too much for him. He had proved to himself time and time again that money couldn't buy happiness. He would think back to the times when he and Alana talked to the launch owners at the marina. They weren't happy, and with all the money they spent on their splendid toys, they still had worries! He just needed to be away from the vineyard and the extravagance that went with it; he needed his own space. When he looked at his brother Ritchie, he wondered how two beings from the same family could be so different. Ritchie was the yuppie, the optimist, and he was the pessimist. In his eyes whatever he or his children wanted had to be earned, not given without any input, but Alana could not accept his thinking, and this was where the marriage collapsed.

The Morrisey girls were born into a privileged lifestyle, so the careers they chose were all tied to the vineyard. All three knew no different than the life they had been part of. This is where their lives began, it was their birthright, so they aimed to continue with the family tradition. Little had they known one of their lives would was be cut short, and the heartache it would bring to the family, but it proved strong family ties could overcome the saddest of times.

When the girls' father looked back over his life, his saddest moment was losing his Briar. She was his shadow, and he thought he had his girls' lives all sorted out for them, but his favourite daughter was the dark horse. He did not foresee a relationship happening under his nose, but with Thomas … why? He could not understand why Briar chose him; was it a father figure she was searching for? He was sad she had not come to him, but how would he have coped if he knew the truth and would he have accepted it? But the heart-wrenching part was no one being with her during her pregnancy, especially the birth of their first grandchild, and this hurt was still with him. James was Briar's legacy, the treasure she gave them all; it was as if she never fully left them. He was the one that would hold the family together, and the family inheritance would be in good hands.

Willow and Ritchie had become well known in the

wine industry, holding tastings at their winery and joining other winemakers in their endeavours to reach the top. Ritchie had developed a good marketing strategy, much to the delight of his father-in-law as he couldn't do the long-distance travel any more. He shared his knowledge with Ritchie as they both knew promotion was the key to selling their wines. It was now his time to travel the world doing the promoting. His first trip was to America to their warehouse base, before Mr Trump made his final decision on the much talked about tariffs. They had arranged for four containers of wine to be shipped to America, hoping they would reach there before the big announcement. Once the tariffs came to bear, the importers had to pay the taxes on their shipments on arrival at US ports, before they could collect their deliveries. It was an upfront tax.

Three weeks had passed before Ritchie could get all his visas sorted for the countries he was intending to visit. It was now April 2025 and the beginning of Mr Trump's 'Liberation Day' trade policy of introducing baseline tariffs of 10 per cent universally. But for New Zealand, like many other countries, the tariffs were to be based on perceived trade imbalances. For this reason, the New Zealand tariff was set at 16 per cent, effective from April 2025. The local winemakers knew they relied upon the US as it was a significant market for New Zealand wine, accounting for approximately 40 per cent of its wine exports, valued at around $NZ800 million annually. They all worried about the long-term impact it would have on the industry, but they would fight it.

For the American economy this was supposedly good,

as it reduced competitors and boosted domestic production. Mr Trump's idea was to return manufacturing to its home country, to force Americans to drink only American wine … taking away their freedom of choice.

Several years ago, at the sudden explosion of vineyards, wine was the favoured alcoholic beverage, but Willow, along with her father, could see a trend of decline and now with the US tariffs would this be a further change in drinking habits. Their Irish outlet was a godsend, but they still relied on their US markets.

The whole dynamics of the wine industry were changing, and Willow was grateful that her father had the vision to set out and secure overseas markets in Europe. Now it was up to her generation to follow in his footsteps, and that meant Ritchie had to step up. As much as he took a long time to earn his father-in-law's respect, he certainly possessed the self-confidence and the ability to win people over; in other words he was a born salesman. Ritchie had put his law career on hold, as now he was fulltime in the vineyard.

Mathew was growing up in a loving environment, and he was the best medicine for Willow as she only ever thought of him as her and Ritchie's son. Her life would have been empty without him. She had a lot to thank Kate for, and she never let Mathew forget his mother.

Life had gone in a full circle. Willow's father didn't get all the grandchildren he planned on, as life had dealt some cruel blows along the way. First losing Briar so young, then Willow's inability to conceive, had quashed the hope of the many grandchildren to carry forward the next generation. He felt for Alana, but he had doubts about the marriage at the onset, and that it lasted as long as it did he felt was a miracle. Timothy was different, and he never accepted the lifestyle that Alana was born into. But the one person he disliked right from the first moment he met was the one who came to the fore and proved him wrong, and that was Ritchie. Was there a bit of himself in Ritchie? Did they clash because they were similar in some ways? He felt the vineyard was in good hands. Willow was always the competitive daughter, and she would carry on pushing her skills to the limit to produce award-winning wines, as it was in her blood.

Thomas was still the workshop manager; he couldn't leave because of all the wonderful memories that he and Briar shared in his workplace. James was his saviour, and if not for him his life would have ended a long time ago, as the pain of losing Briar would have been too great for him to bear.

The legacy for the vineyard was Willow's award-winning wine, Harvest of Hearts.' This told the story of the three sisters, their lives, their highs and lows, and the bond that held them together, to continue with their parents' dream.

The future lay in the capable hands of James, Jessica, her sister and Mathew, the new generation who would carry on the family legacy.

About the Author

Margaret Nyhon is a New Zealand novelist living in Mosgiel, Dunedin. Margaret has written more than a dozen novels spanning multiple genres, including historical and romance as well as contemporary thrillers. She also has written a book of modern verse focusing on well-being and world affairs. Her first book, *de Marisco,* was a non-fiction work tracing her family history. This is what set Margaret on her writing career and the researching has never stopped.

Contact Margaret: margaretf@hotmail.co.nz

Other books by the author

Fiction

Isobella (Book 1 in the *Isobella* series)

Isobella: Self Redemption (Book 2 in the *Isobella* series)

Papa's Girl Emmeline

Betrayal by an Irish Rose

Revenge for an English Lord (sequel to *Betrayal by an Irish Rose*)

For Girls' Eyes Only

Daughters Lost to the Underworld

Pimchan and Amira

Coronavirus: A Novel

The Whistle-blower's Severed Link (sequel to *Coronavirus: A Novel*)

Fortune Smiles as Love Divides

The Stolen Girl (sequel to *Fortune Smiles as Love Divides*)

My Past Became My Present

Non-fiction

de Marisco

Freedom Knows No Boundaries

A Wake-up Call

A Shattered Dream Across the Tasman

Memories and Moving On

www.ingramcontent.com/pod-product-compliance
Lightning Source LLC
Chambersburg PA
CBHW030338310726
48979CB00001B/94